Hot,
Hard &
Howling

MARI
FREEMAN

ELLORA'S CAVE
ROMANTICA®
WWW.ELLORASCAVE.COM

An Ellora's Cave Publication

www.ellorascave.com

Hot, Hard & Howling

ISBN 9781419965234
ALL RIGHTS RESERVED.
Hot, Hard & Howling Copyright © 2011 Mari Freeman
Edited by Kelli Collins.
Design by Syneca.

Electronic book publication March 2011
Trade paperback publication 2011

HOT, HARD & HOWLING

ഇ

Dedication

ഉ

For my aunt Martha, who took seven years to finish her only novel. Through illness, blindness and loss of her true love, she got the words on paper any way she could. She never stopped writing.

Acknowledgements

ഉ

This book was a long time in coming. I think it was five years ago that the idea first came to mind. Life jumped in, other things become more pressing and then a fire destroyed the outline and notes for the series. When I finally sat back down to spend some time with Nell and Trent, a whole new world bubbled up in my head. It just goes to show, everything turns out the way it's supposed to.

Many thanks to Tricia for your thoughts and ideas, as well as the yard full of kids' stuff that bought me some quiet time.

Chapter One

ဆ

Naked, covered in blood and with a dead human on the bathroom floor was not exactly how one wanted to greet guests. Exasperated, Nell tossed the toothbrush aside. All the scrubbing in the world wasn't going to get that blood out.

She looked in the mirror. Curly golden hair hung wild after drying on its own as she'd tried to save the grout. Her face was still flushed from the struggle and the scrubbing. Her cheeks and chin were scratched and bloody. The scratches didn't matter. Small wounds healed quickly for a half-Demon. Nell rubbed with her fingers to try to get smears of blood off her face. She looked around for her robe and found it lying under the dead guy's shoulder. Nell snorted. "Great."

She scanned the rest of the contents of the vanity. Nothing of use left. She'd tried all the cleansers under the sink and none of them were getting the rust-colored stains out. Her gaze crossed the floor. At least the pool of blood there would come up with no problem. She propped her hands on her hips. "Damn."

"What's going on up there?" Her sister's voice rang from the living room. "I had a funky vision." Sonja lived several miles up the mountain. How had she gotten there so fast?

"And of course you rushed right over." Vision? Great. Nell and both her younger sisters were half-Demon, so their Demon powers were unpredictable at best. The curse of the Halflings, their mi-ma always said. Even their shifts were only partial.

When Sonja had visions, everyone was wary of the information contained within. The crazy things were so confusing that no one, including Sonja herself, could decipher the images. Evidently this one had been clear enough to send Sonja out into the night to come check on Nell. Hadn't the girl ever heard of a phone?

Nell found a dirty t-shirt hanging from a hook on the back of the bathroom door and pulled it on. "Up here. Did you bring bleach?"

"Bleach?" Sonja's voice was closer. She stopped at the entrance of the bathroom. "Oh. You know, I almost did." She bent over the fetal body on the floor to get a better look. "Nell," she gasped, shooting straight up. "He's human!"

"Duh. Do you smell blood magic? I smelled it when he attacked, but since I started trying to save the shower grout, I lost track of the scent."

Sonja raised her eyebrow. "Blood magic? Really? How would a human have the smell of that?" She stepped over the body, looking down at the object sticking out of the man's chest. "Is that a…"

Nell cleared her throat and let out an exasperated breath. "Yeah."

Sonja bit her lip but failed in her attempt to hold back a loud, barking laugh. "You killed a man with a *dildo*?"

With that, Sonja lost control over her laughter and let it roll. Tears leaked from her eyes as she leaned against the wall for support.

Nell straightened her spine. "It was close by," she protested, gesturing wildly at the dead man. "And I think the scissors actually killed him." So what? Everybody had toys. She just happened to have a very large collection. "I was in the shower. I had to use what was close."

Nell's Demon gift of telekinesis was as inconsistent as Sonja's visions and the ramifications were much more immediate when things went amiss. Sometimes she would move the wrong thing or a power surge would send objects hurling off at the speed of…well, a flying dildo. The toy had been on the counter, among other things, and it had just flown with everything else when she'd blasted her power at the attacker.

"You use those things in the shower? God, Nell. You are the strangest woman."

"I wasn't using it in the shower. I cleaned it *before* I got in the shower. Don't you clean yours?"

Nell was the wild one, the extrovert, the only one of the three sisters who had truly ventured out into the world. She had traveled, explored and experienced things she wouldn't ever be able to explain to her younger sisters. Her collection of sex toys came from all over the world, even a few from other realms. The piece currently sticking out of the chest of the human man on her floor was one of her favorites. A beautiful work of art. She'd gotten it from the leader of a Demon sect in India.

"Death by dildo!" Sonja laughed. "Oh my, Nell. The Prime is going to have a field day with this."

"Shut up." Nell plopped down on the closed toilet lid with her bloody knees pushed together. She let her head drop into her hands. She didn't want to see the Prime. Not yet. "Did you call Mi-ma?"

Sonja smiled at her. "Yep. On her way over, and *she's* already contacted the Prime."

Nell pulled herself off the toilet and started to pick up the scattered mess, snatching up her makeup, another causality of the assault. When she'd used her telekinesis to throw things at her attacker, she hadn't paid much attention to what went flying. Thus the very long, very ornate dildo currently lodged between his ribs. Maybe if she could extract it before the Prime arrived…

"Stop, Nell. You killed a human. Blood magic on him or not, you have to report it and you shouldn't touch the scene." The tone in her sister's voice stopped Nell in her tracks. The sudden change from amusement to panic made Nell want to curse again. "You know the rules."

Yeah, Nell knew the rules. They all knew the rules. The rules were jackhammered into the brain of every supernatural being from their time of birth or creation. The rules were all part of keeping the magical world a secret and keeping peace between supernatural species. And rule number one was, if you hurt a human, even in self-defense, it had to be reported to the Council of Preternatural Code and a Prime Investigator would come a-calling.

The Primes were like cops, but they could also be judge, jury and hangman if the situation warranted. It wasn't the *consequences* Nell didn't want to face. It was *him*. Trent Nicholas, the Prime for the area.

She needed more time. She hadn't come up with a good plan yet. Even after years of cavorting with some very powerful and amazing creatures, Nell's knees got weak and other things got moist when Trent was around. The lack of control really pissed her off. She considered it a serious deficiency.

"I can't smell the blood magic anymore," Nell said as she paced into the hall. "I can't prove it. This guy attacked me and someone or something put him up to it. Do you think the high-and-mighty Trenton Nicholas is going to listen to me?"

"Calm down. This is his job we're talking about. He won't be such an ass while he's working." Sonja hesitated. "Well...*maybe* he won't be." She gave Nell a meager smile. "Okay, he'll be an ass, but we still have to report it." Sonja headed down the stairs. "Don't move anything else. Come on down and I'll make tea and we'll figure all this out."

Nell looked around her wrecked bathroom. The blood would come off the walls and the tub and sink, but she still worried about the old grout. She paused in the doorway to look over the body once more. She didn't recognize the man splayed on her floor. Didn't know why he would attack her in her own home. She lived out in the woods, in her father's old cabin. When he died last year, she had inherited the place. Her sisters got chunks of money and artifacts, but Nell had always wanted the house. It reminded her of Dad at every turn. It still smelled like him. His things still sat where he'd left them. The master bedroom she'd made her own. The rest she'd left as if he still lived here.

After traveling the world for years, she was more than happy to settle back in the woods of North Carolina and just be home and quiet for a while. The back deck overlooked the side of Grandfather Mountain, so there were no lights from the city to block her view of the stars at night. She loved it here. She loved the solitude, the connection to nature.

She glanced down at the dead guy. So much for quiet.

The doorbell rang as she headed down the stairs. Sonja beat her to it.

* * * * *

Trent stood stock still as Sonja flung the door open to him without a care.

Nell Ambercroft was standing on the stairs that flowed into the living room, half-dressed and half-covered in blood. The sight of her stirred him. He had expected it, but not this quickly and not so strong. He bit his tongue to keep from rushing to her.

Nell complained, "Jeez, Sonja, do ya think you could have checked to see who it was, considering..." The bloody half-Demon motioned to her disheveled state.

"Well, who else would be out here at three in the morning but Mi-ma or him?" Sonja gestured to Trent. Neither had actually greeted him. "Relax, sis."

"Relax? *Relax*? I swear. You don't know who it could have been. Someone sent that guy here. What if it had been another crazy trying to kill me?"

"How likely is that?" Sonja asked, drawing her eyebrows together and putting her hands on her hips, still completely ignoring Trent. "The guy in the bathroom has only been dead, what, thirty minutes? Do you think his boss or whatever has even had time to realize he's gone?"

Nell took two more steps down. "What if he had a partner? Goddess knows what could have been hiding in the woods."

"Would a murderer ring the bell?"

Gritting his teeth, Trent Nicholas stood and watched the discourse between the sisters. Nothing changed with this family. They were all nuts; Demon nuts, to top it off. He was the Prime for three states and if that wasn't enough to command respect, he was a high-ranking Werewolf in this community. Finding himself ignored by these two Halflings was just about more than he could take.

He let his gaze drift past Sonja and back up the stairs once more. As much as he hated it, Nell had always awakened his wolf. For years she had lurked in his fantasies. Tales of her travels, of her living in a Vamp nest in Paris or convincing a Demon in Scotland to take her across several realms, haunted his dreams. Moons only knew what else the woman had gotten up to. She was a wild thing.

There she stood, arguing and animated, wearing only a tiny shirt that barely covered her. Trent could easily make out her curves and he clenched his fists as his wolf growled in appreciation of her form. She wasn't a Hollywood beauty. Far from it, even a little on the short side, but that did nothing to diminish the wildness of her personality, which shone through her skin and sparkled in her eyes.

A mane of golden-blonde curls hung slightly past her shoulders and highlighted eyes the color of a fawn's coat. A lush brown that darkened as she got angry, Trent noticed. Her legs were well shaped and the shirt almost let him get a look at what he was sure would be paradise. Somehow the little Halfling got to him on a far deeper level than he was comfortable with. He'd fought it, and had hoped the time they had spent apart would cool his desire. It hadn't. Nell made him want things that could only lead to disaster.

12

He eyed the blood drying on her legs, arms and face. There was none on the outside of the shirt. He deduced she had put it on after the incident. He would love to ask, but they wouldn't—

"Shut up!"

"Trent Nicholas, don't you have any manners?" Sonja asked, her eyes widening at his tone.

Trent raised his eyebrows at the little imp. Manners? Who gave a shit about manners at a time like this? "Where's the body?" he all but growled at Nell, ignoring the woman at his side.

Nell looked at Sonja. "You make the tea." She shooed her sister into the kitchen then descended the rest of the stairs. "Bathroom." She motioned for him to enter and stood her ground until he passed. He'd really been hoping to follow her up the stairs and get a peek under that shirt.

In the bathroom, Trent looked over the scene. Makeup, hair stuff and all manner of girl things were strewn over the floor, some under and some on top of the blood. The human lay on his side facing away, with his feet close to the tub and his head by the door. He looked over the splatter on the walls and the pool on the floor.

The clean spot on the far wall confused him. "You tried to clean the shower?"

"I wanted it off the old grout before it stained. As you can see, I failed." She was leaning against the doorframe, letting him have the run of the bathroom. The rooms in the house were very large, even the bath. Then again, her father had been a very big boy in his Demon form.

Trent nodded at her and reached to turn the body. He pulled the human by the shoulder and rolled him onto his back. Lodged in the ribs of the man looked to be...

He blinked his eyes to make sure he was seeing correctly. "Is that—"

"Yes. It is." Nell cut him off. "If you have one thing to say, Trenton Nicholas…" She didn't finish the threat.

He held back a wave of laughter as he watched her face tighten and her eyes darken. "You were in the shower when the human came in?" He tilted the man's head to see the small pair of scissors sticking out of his neck. Probably the killing blow, but Trent would use the dildo to get a rise out of her. He smiled to himself—and then frowned as he imagined Nell, naked and wet. He had no trouble picturing her bracing herself with one hand against the tile, her head thrown back in the throes of passion, that toy rubbing in just the right way between her spread thighs. He cleared his throat. "You use those things in the shower?"

"It's none of your business where I use those things," she huffed as she scratched absently at the blood on her arms.

Sonja stuck her head in. "You should see her collection, Trent. It's quite extensive. Sex toys from all around the world and then some."

"Don't you have to go home?" Nell bent and rubbed the tops of her thighs.

"No."

Trent hoped they would argue for a few minutes. It would give him a chance to look around the bathroom and time to get his aching erection to calm down. Maybe the Halfling could handle his animal side after all. If the size of that dildo was any indication, she was more than capable. Casually, he tried to adjust his jeans as he looked for any weapons the human may have carried.

"Nell," he said, interrupting the sisters, "what did he attack you with? Did he have a weapon?"

She huffed and leaned back against the wall, rubbing roughly at her stomach. "That was the strangest thing. I felt someone here, sensed him, right before he yanked open the shower curtain. I'm not all that sensitive to magic but I felt his presence. Then I smelled the blood magic. It wasn't strong but

14

it was there. I was using jasmine soap and I could smell that stink over the jasmine right before he grabbed at the curtain and started babbling about a puzzle box. Scared the crap out of me. Then I saw the knife. It was glowing, as if it were red hot. But as soon as I started flinging stuff, I got him with the...ah...I got him in the chest. Anyway, as soon as he was hit, the knife disappeared. I've never seen anything like it."

"Knife must have been spelled." Trent nodded. "Probably the human too."

Nell pulled herself away from the wall. "So, you don't think I killed him on purpose?"

"Why should I? Looks like you defended yourself." Trent glanced around the room again, using his keen sense of smell. "It was an elaborate attack, Nell. You know any reason a master Sorcerer would use blood magic against you?"

Her bright eyes widened. "Master?"

"Smells that way to me." Trent could still catch hints of the magic. "Only a master could weave a spell strong enough to influence a human yet leave so small a trace." He paced the cavernous room briefly then stopped, facing Nell again. "What about the puzzle box? Any clue what that meant?"

He realized Nell wasn't listening to him any longer. She was looking down at the blood on her legs and arms, trying to rub it off. The mostly dried blood seemed to be causing a reaction, attacking her skin. He watched, stunned, as the clinging streaks seemed to become animated, looking as if they were writhing on her body. Rubbing harder only managed to smear them.

Nell's skin was starting to pinken from the rubbing as her efforts became more frantic, her scrubbing fingers moving from her arms to her legs and back.

A look of panic took over her delicate features. Her complexion darkened and her eyes took on a golden glow. The parts of her skin not covered in blood started to shimmer, giving him a peek at her Demon. The last thing he needed was a Halfling taking on Demon form unintentionally.

Trent had heard of complicated spells that could taint blood, but he'd never seen one in action. He was mesmerized by her partial change as her Demon started to surface. What looked like a Dragon—angry and pained—appeared as a mere shadow under her skin. As a Werewolf, he understood a body's *physical* change, but she was becoming golden from within. It was very different from the bone-crunching shift he underwent, much more fluid, graceful.

Trent shook himself inwardly. Seeing her stronger Demon side stirred even deeper desires he'd hidden away.

"Bring her downstairs!" Sonja screeched as she realized what was happening. "The blood's spelled. Prime, help her!"

The use of his title and the pleading in Sonja's tone snapped Trent out of his thoughts and he scooped up the now fully panicked Halfling.

"Get it off! Hell's fire, get it off!" Tears trailed down Nell's cheeks as she clawed at her own skin. She was in real pain—and he was standing there without a clue how to help.

Her shirt had ridden up so Trent got a good view of her exposed mound. He cursed himself for looking while she was in such distress. Sonja pushed him toward the door. Forward movement. That he could do. He concentrated on the stairs to keep his mind where it belonged. "Easy, girl. It's okay." The words were a piss-poor attempt at comfort, but comfort wasn't his forte. He was a Prime, a Werewolf and a triggerman, not a nurturer.

At the bottom of the stairs, Sonja pushed past him. "There's a pond in the garden. I need to get some stuff from the kitchen. Put her in the water. It'll soothe her some. Do *not* take her out of that water until I get there."

He glanced back upstairs, toward the shower. It had water, was closer and seemed easier than the pond.

16

Sonja read his mind. "No. It has to be the pond. It's blessed and natural. Do you understand?"

Trent nodded and carried a squirming Nell down a short hall, through the kitchen and out the back door of the cabin.

The deck in the back opened out onto a large kitchen garden. Metal lanterns with white candles magically lit themselves in response to his presence as he hurried down the only path away from the house. He rounded a bend and saw the pond. As he approached, more candles lit. Their reflections sparkled across the still, black water. The effect mirrored the stars in the clear night. The first-quarter moon was high. He felt it pull at his wolf as he sniffed for any surrounding danger.

Trent didn't hesitate at the pond's edge. He walked into the water, holding her like a groom would carry his bride. He did his level best to hold Nell steady even as she continued to claw at her legs. Angry red marks were starting to appear on her thighs. When he got deep enough that buoyancy held much of her weight, he captured her wrists with one hand and braced her body against his with the other.

"Shhhh. Nell. Look at me." He watched as she turned her tear-soaked face toward him. The anguish there touched him deeper than he wanted to examine at the moment. He rocked her gently until she finally quit squirming. Letting go of her hands, he pushed her hair out of her face. "You'll hurt yourself, little one." She was still whimpering, almost weightless against him, calmer but still trembling in his arms. He splashed water over her thighs and rubbed over the reddened skin with a light touch. The tainted blood, unaffected by the cleansing water, was raised like an old scar on her soft skin. He rubbed a little harder.

"It won't come off without a healing spell. Dark magic, tainted blood, it's like acid." She sniffed and wiped her face with the heel of her palm. "If I'd worried about the blood instead of the tile and washed it right away…"

"Is this permanent?" he asked, hoping not. It was all over her thighs, arms and that beautiful face. He hated the thought of all her golden skin marred by scars. He continued to rub her thigh gently.

"Mi-ma will call our friend Clara. She's not a master but she's a powerful coven leader." She rested her head on his shoulder.

This was the actual attack. He knew it in his bones. "Nell, do you have any idea who might have wanted to hurt you like this?"

"I'd never seen the guy before."

He readjusted her in the water, making sure her arms were still submerged. Even under the water he could feel the heat coming off her skin. "I mean the blood. I think the human was a setup. He was sacrificed. He was *meant* to be injured by your...gift."

Nell wrinkled her brow at him and came very close to a smile. "You mean the mayhem I cause when I use my Demon skills?"

"I think the tainted blood was the real attack. You could have defended yourself easily against a human, even with your limited control. Someone wanted to send you a message or hurt you, Nell. Is there anyone from your past, your travels, who would want to scar you like this?" He nodded to her thighs. Her shirt was almost up to her breasts and he realized not only were her legs and arms marked by the tainted blood, but so was her stomach. They had timed it just right, attacking her in the shower.

"If the Witch can't cleanse the blood, the scars and the burning will be with me forever," Nell responded. Without modesty, she ran her hand over her stomach.

Trent tried to think of the master Sorcerers he knew in the area. The list wasn't long, there weren't too many of them out there. He'd need to call in a few favors, find out if there were any new masters in the area recently. Master Sorcerers were incredibly powerful and easily tempted to use blood magic to boost their influence.

He pulled her a little tighter against his chest. She was irritatingly half-Demon, but she still felt like all woman against him. A beautiful woman, one he'd hoped never to see in pain again...

Trent had hurt her. Years ago. He'd pushed her away. They'd still been kids, really, and he'd done it publically, embarrassing her with his rejection. For years he'd regretted it. But it was the way things had to be. She was an energetic, vibrant woman. A mate like Nell would push him past his limit. After all, he was his father's son. And Trent had no intention of following in his father's obsessive, abusive paw prints. A night or two was all he could ever offer Nell. That was it. She deserved better. It was true way back then and it was true now.

He hardened his resolve and reminded his aching cock of his pledge. The darn thing was *not* listening. He felt it, hot and hard, straining against wet denim as he stood in the cool water. He searched his memories for something to get his mind off her body.

"So, you really lived in a Vampire nest in Paris?"

She arched a wet, weary eyebrow at him. "For a while."

"Are they as wild as we hear?" He cursed himself for the direction he'd unintentionally taken the conversation. Some of the Vamp nests were little more than bordellos for any and all paranormal beings who showed up. Places where all sorts of cravings were catered to, with few limits or taboos. The one Nell had joined was more of a spiritual commune. He had checked. Oh, he was sure there was lots of sex, but that wasn't the basis of that particular nest.

She shifted in the water. The movement brushed her breast against his arm. A soft moan escaped her lips. "They can be. I lived with a tamer group but all Vampires have deep, needful appetites."

He smiled down at her. "That where you started your collection?"

19

She shook her head and gave him a teasing smile, then gritted her teeth and gripped his forearm. "Nope. That started long before. Mi-ma bought my first one, years ago, after my ego was crushed by some arrogant Werewolf who left me with a broken heart and raging hormones."

He laughed aloud. How could she say that with a straight face? "You stretch the truth, I think."

"My kitten *never* tells tales, young man. Being Prime has gone to your head," Mi-ma declared loudly from behind them as she marched toward the edge of the pond.

Chapter Two

ഇ

Trent stopped laughing. Two people had come upon the pond, as well as Sonja, and he had been so distracted by Nell and her toy collection that he hadn't heard or smelled their approach.

He looked at the old lady he had known all his life. She was one of the few left in town who'd known his mother and how she'd died. The round, old Demon was a bit addled, in his opinion. Her tightly curled salt-and-pepper hair looked as though she never brushed it. She also walked with a limp and the story she told when they were kids was that she'd tangled with a lion in *her* day. Trent still felt like a child in Mi-ma's presence.

"Yes, I started her collection. You can never have too many toys." She hesitated and looked back over her shoulder to the woman behind her. "Or men, for that matter." The woman laughed and Mi-ma turned back to the pair in the water. "I got her one just last year. A toy, that is. It was an onyx phallus from the vault of Nefertiti herself. Quite a valuable piece. I believe the carving is most lifelike." She removed and dropped the scarf from around her neck. "Her father brought her one back from South America that would put to shame a big, strong Werewolf like you."

With that, Trent felt his cheeks color, hearing such blatant talk from the woman who'd helped him with math homework as a child.

He didn't recognize the scrawny Vamp who was giggling just behind Mi-ma. Sonja was biting her lip to keep quiet. He even felt Nell tremble with laughter in his arms. Trent couldn't stop himself from letting a small chuckle go at his own

21

expense. This night was just plain weird and as a Prime, an agent for the Council that regulates the supernatural world, that was really saying something. These women were all nuts.

An older woman Trent knew as the local coven leader joined the crew on the edge of the pond. She didn't speak as she opened a satchel and started spreading out the tools of her craft. Mi-ma made her way into the water without a care to her clothes. She tsked and tenderly cupped Nell's cheek.

All the humor in her eyes was gone as she studied her granddaughter. "Be strong, my brave girl. Does it pain you much?" Trent was moved by the loving way she touched Nell. "Has his touch soothed?"

"It's not so bad, Mi, the Prime has actually taken good care of his charge." He listened to the women talk as though he would have done differently. Did the Demons think him so cold that he wouldn't help ease her pain the best he could?

The old woman tapped his chin with the same hand that had touched Nell's face. "He'll do. He'll do just fine."

He looked back to Nell but she had closed her eyes. He didn't like feeling confused and Mi-ma always had that effect on him, often speaking in unconnected bursts, blurting out odd premonitions. He looked to the Witch who was still kneeling and hunched over her work on the bank. "Can you stop the scarring?"

"Yes, but wolf, the greatest help will come from you, if you're willing." She straightened from her task and made steady eye contact with him.

"Me? What can I do?"

Mi-ma chuckled. "She needs some strong, clean blood to cleanse the taint, wolf. Ours is too close to hers. Even Clara," she gestured to the Witch with a splash, "is too closely related to offer a strong cleansing. Yours is the strongest blood here, will do the most good to heal those blisters. But I brought our neighbor, David, to do it if you're not willing to give up the blood of the wolf."

22

Trent looked at the stringy Vamp hovering in the background. His wolf growled inside his head. There was no way Nell was taking any blood from *that*, but exchanging blood was a very serious thing to the pack.

He hesitated. Nell's body relaxed in his arms; she was losing her fight to stay conscious.

He'd known this woman since she was a child and, even though he couldn't have a relationship with her, he'd give her what he could, his essence, his life force. He just hoped he could resist her once she carried his scent.

"Relax, wolf-boy," Sonja said. "Most of it will be *on* her. She only has to take a little inside. We know what blood exchange means to you."

Nell squirmed, struggled to open her eyes. "Don't manipulate him like that, Sonja. I can take it from David. Just get on with it."

David moved forward. Trent growled. His body, his wolf, was roaring at him to keep the Vamp away from the woman in his arms. He took a step back with her.

Mi-ma turned, heading toward the edge of the pond. "Just as I thought. Are you ready, Clara?" The Witch nodded, attention already back on her task of mixing who knows what in a copper bowl. Mi-ma lowered her voice. "Trenton. Bring her to the bank of the pond."

Trent huffed. He was acting as though Nell were his mate. It was just because Nell was being threatened. He didn't like it at all, any of it. She might only need a little of his blood, but it only took a little for his wolf or any others from his pack to recognize the mark. He forced his legs to move. Nell hissed as her arms left the water. He bent his knees to keep her under the cool liquid as long as possible as he moved forward.

He placed her in the circle the Witch had drawn and blessed to the goddesses. Trent stayed by her side, watching helplessly as she writhed, her nails digging into her own skin.

"Can you hurry?" Nell whimpered.

23

The Witch started up her chant and held out her hand. Palm up, Trent placed his hand in hers. Trent didn't flinch as the Witch cut a small slice in the meaty part of his palm. Nell was getting pale, her face tight with a pain much deeper than his. The chanting rose to a high, fevered rhythm as Mi-ma and Sonja joined in. Clara tilted his palm, letting blood drip into the copper bowl with the herbs. She took Nell's sweating hand, pried her tight fist open and placed a small cut on her palm as well, letting only two drops fall into the bowl. He expected the potion to hiss or boil, but only a stale bloody smell wafted in the still night.

Clara cut off Nell's shirt, leaving her naked and shaking. Gently, she worked the potion into the worst of the red streaks, which had started to look like fresh burns. She started at Nell's shoulders, moving tenderly down each arm, chanting softly as she stroked. Her hands kept a steady motion of slow circles that mimicked the cadence of the chant as she covered Nell's breasts and then her stomach, over the hips and finally down her legs to her feet. Nell continued to squirm in pain as Clara finished her journey over her body.

Trent was worried that it hadn't worked. "Was my blood not strong enough?"

"Patience, boy," Clara said, and pulled Nell into a sitting position, resting her against Trent's side. The Witch held the bowl to Nell's lips, pushed her thumb into Nell's mouth to get her to open her lips and tilted the bowl. Nell sputtered then took a sip. Once she got a little into her mouth, she leaned into the bowl, trying eagerly to take more. The bigger gulp gagged her, making her jerk away, spitting. Then her eyes rolled back, her head fell forward and her entire little body shivered violently before finally falling still. Trent wrapped his arms around her.

"Trent." Sonja's voice pulled barely his attention away from Nell. "Can you get her back to her bedroom?"

He nodded and picked up the limp body of the woman he had always thought of as impossibly alive. The sight of her unconscious made him feel things he knew he would always have to deny. The scent of his blood mingling with hers had his wolf moaning in agony at her lifeless state. He ground his teeth and took a steadying breath. He would feel better after they cleaned her up and he got some distance away. But now, at this moment, his wolf wanted her, her blood, her body, and it wanted to mate. He had all but performed the mating ritual by offering his blood. The circumstances were different from a traditional mating ceremony, but his wolf didn't know that. The wolf knew there was a naked female it desired in Trent's arms, and the wolf wanted to take her, bind her.

Trent fought his natural urges as he ascended the stairs. He would never mate. That would be a disaster. His obsessive, jealous nature was too strong to deal with her outgoing personality. History would repeat itself and he could never let that happen. He could never destroy this woman the way his father had destroyed his mother. It was best to get away from here, away from *her*.

As he passed the bathroom, he realized an immediate exit was impossible. He had to remove the human, and that meant staying close to Nell. Gently, he laid Nell's unresponsive, bloody body on her bed. The others had followed and were filing into the room. He backed away and blocked the door with his body as the Vamp started to enter. A skinny young Vamp was no match for a strong Were, much less one who was also a Prime. David changed directions and muttered something about tea.

When Trent turned his attention back to the bed, the women were covering Nell with a sheet, making no effort to clean off the blood or the remains of the potion. Their faces were drawn and worried. He stayed by the door, wet and dripping on the floor, his wolf pressing to escape, his muscles twitching and the hair on the back of his neck itchy. "How long until you know if that worked?"

Mi-ma came to him as Sonja lay by Nell's side and started singing to her in a low voice, gently running her fingers through her sister's tangled, wet hair. "She will wake by tomorrow. If your gift was true, wolf, she will be healed." She looked him over. Her nose wrinkled as if she smelled something bad. "Go. Run the woods. I feel the change on you from here. It's safe. We'll clean the mess in the bathroom and have the human ready for you when you return."

He didn't understand how the old Demon sensed his change, especially so far from a full moon. But then, thinking back, he had rarely understood her. It was unusual for Demons to be able to sense such things and he and his cousins had always suspected Mi-ma was something else. She'd been around forever and no one knew her origins. Mi-ma was like family to everyone on the mountain. She just...*was.*

He nodded and Mi-ma grasped his forearm before he could leave the room. "The past, young man, is never as it seems, and usually best not used to shape the future."

Trent started to tell Mi-ma she didn't know shit about his past, but thought better of it. She probably knew more than most, but it didn't matter. *All* he had to go on was the past. Ignoring history was too risky.

Trent realized he would have never made it through the cleanup. The smell of the victim's blood, mingled with Nell's and his own, would have been too much. His wolf was growling, stretching, reaching for the surface, hungry to take the woman lying upstairs covered in his blood. Hungry to mate.

Trent peeled off his damp clothes outside, letting them fall to the wood decking with a heavy splat before pausing to inhale the fresh mountain air. Exhaling, he took two running steps and let the change take his body as he left the deck. Four paws hit the pine-straw-covered earth instead of two feet. Fire ran through his veins as he took off in a gallop past the pond, out of the light cast by the burning lanterns, the beast urging him to mate as he ran free in the forest to escape the call.

* * * * *

Crey shifted nervously as he eyed the beautiful young Witch who sprawled naked and unconscious in the disheveled bed against the wall. She looked as if she'd been used hard. Her skin was still pink, glistening. He'd seen a lot of dead bodies and this one was defiantly alive, her nipples still hard. The bitch was even aroused after she'd been fucked into oblivion. Impressive. He'd heard stories about the Palero Priest and his abilities with the women. The Palero, with his dark looks and high status, could sway almost any creature into his bed.

Crey would never hold that kind of power over women. He preferred to force his companions to relieve his tensions. The thought made him just a little hard. He glanced around the room and realized he could take *this* one while she was still out and she'd never know. His eyes perused the sleeping Witch's generous curves. The priest liked his women with a little more padding than Crey preferred. He'd fuck her anyway, beggars and choosers and all…

Why had the bastard left him here with this kind of temptation? If he touched her, the evil one would hex him for sure. Still, his blood was thickening. His arousal growing.

Crey shuffled again. Self-control was not his strong suit. He took a tentative step toward the bed. The Witch shifted, exposing more of her curves. The smell of sex filled the air around him. He could care less that most of that smell was from another man—if Paleros were still men at all. It'd been a while since he'd thrust into an unwilling victim, and he wanted to now.

He was about to let himself indulge when he felt the Palero's energy coming. The black magic was so strong Crey felt it itching in the back of his conscious thoughts before he could see him in the hall. It made him feel nauseous for a moment.

The feeling helped him gather his thoughts and he quickly stepped away from the bed.

"Wise decision," the Palero said, his voice as appealing as his chiseled face. Crey was still horny, and needed to control his libido before the priest had *him* unconscious in that bed next to the Witch...with a sore ass. Paleros' appetites were fierce and they gave little care for whom or what they used to slake them.

The Santeria priest was a specialist of African Voodoo and Crey suspected he was one of the most powerful creatures on the planet. There was nothing or no one more evil, of that Crey was sure. But Crey wanted out of the bargain he'd struck. Ten years had been long enough. He was tired of doing all the Palero's dirty work. And he had a plan to get out from under the priest's thumb.

"Yes. I'm sure it was." He backed away a few more steps and bowed humbly to acknowledge the fact that the priest had determined his intentions with the Witch. "I need more, sir. More of your power." He bowed his head farther without taking his eyes completely off the beautiful man.

"You botched a very simple job by trying to do magic that was out of your league," the priest replied. He turned to the open window at the far end of the room and lit a cigar. The smoke twisted in the shape of serpents and wound around his head before dissipating into the darkness. "And you want more?"

The Palero turned back to Crey. His green eyes displayed his anger as glowing irises narrowed and became vertical slits. "You killed a human and you left traces of *my* magic on him."

Crey stumbled back into the wall. The Palero's words felt like a blow to the chest. "Forgive me." He struggled to breathe as the pressure increased in his chest. "I thought that using the human would keep us both in the clear." The pressure was now so strong that he thought his ribs would snap and implode. "Was wrong..." Painfully wrong. He watched through blurring vision as, across the room, the Palero gave him a little grin. "You are a beautiful creature even when angry, sir."

28

The Palero laughed out loud and Crey felt the pressure leave his chest. He sucked in hard as his knees buckled. The feel of precious air stung his lungs as it rushed in, the smell of black licorice infiltrated his nose.

He lay on the floor, coughing and sputtering, his lungs burning, and knew the Palero would just as soon kill him as deal with his incompetence. Crey also knew his own weaknesses. Heck, he used them whenever possible, even played them up on occasion. A simple Sorcerer, yes, but he was crafty. Letting people think he was stupid often worked in his favor.

Today would be no different. He would leave with what he needed to get the necklace.

Once he had *that* in his possession, he would be powerful enough to break the hex that held him as one of the pawns in the Palero's many chess games.

He looked up to find the Palero towering over him. "You just earned another life. Don't waste it."

Crey closed his eyes to avoid direct contact with the Palero's stare. "You're a generous man. I could always tell." He looked over to the bed. Part of him hoped the priest would let him have what was left of the Witch, part of him suddenly wanted to *be* her.

"Generosity has nothing to do with it, Crey. You amuse me. But keep in mind that I will find an equal amount of amusement in your destruction. Sorcerers can linger on for years, Crey, stuck between realms, not actually living, not exactly dead. I would find *that* amusing, possibly more so than your bumbling antics." The Palero turned and walked back to the still-burning cigar left on the window ledge. The Palero took a long drag off the stogie. "You owe me for this failure."

Crey sat up. "I'll have it soon."

The Palero opened a cabinet over his wet bar and rummaged through a box. He tossed Crey a gris-gris consisting of burlap pouches tied in a pattern along a thin hemp rope.

"Last opportunity."

Chapter Three

ഔ

The house was quiet when Trent returned. He'd spent the night in his wolf form, high on a ridge that dropped dramatically to the valley below. It was the perfect spot. He could see for miles and the rocky ridge behind him made for good protection. His wolf had been restless, however...wanting. Trent fought for an hour or so of fitful sleep. When he closed his eyes, she was there, the pained look on her face taunting him, making his possessive—no, *obsessive* side roar. He wanted to be with her, protecting her, shielding her.

Her youngest sister, Trina, didn't stop him as he entered the house from the back deck. She was watching TV with the volume low, the colored lights from the images dancing over the walls. She gave him a tilt of the head to send him on up the stairs. She looked tired.

He looked carefully through the bedroom door, expecting a hoard of Halfling women to be surrounding Nell's bed. He found her asleep, her face back to its golden tan, her honey-blonde hair clean and draped neatly to one side, shining against the white sheets. No sign on her face or shoulders of the angry red marks from the attack. He looked into the bathroom. The body was gone. Perfumes, makeup and other bottles and tubes were neatly lined up. The smell of jasmine lingered lightly in the air and the grout was sparkling white. No doubt Mi-ma had something to do with that.

He turned back to the bed and his stomach tightened as he gazed at the angel lying in it.

Angel? Where did that come from?

He wanted to move closer, to confirm that all those angry welts and blisters were truly gone, to know his blood had saved her from an enduring pain. He stepped into the huge room and inched to the side of the door, not toward her or the bed. He felt like a voyeur. Simply watching her sleep was just as powerful as the images he'd had of her in the shower, playing with that dildo. His cock was hard and his wolf was once again restless.

He bumped into the dresser and several things rattled and fell. He tried to right the candles but only managed to knock over something else and he fought an exasperated laugh. Here he was, lurking and nervous in a woman's bedroom. When was the last time he was nervous about anything, much less a troublesome Demon Halfling?

It was the shimmer of the carving that first caught his eye, not the actual shape of the object. Even so, his curiosity carried him over to the ornate chest in the corner of the room. Displayed prominently above the chest, on a small glass shelf halfway up the wall, was an intricately crafted onyx dildo. It must have been the one Mi-ma had mentioned. He was by no means an expert on the subject, but the artisanship that went into this particular *piece* was evident. He leaned closer but resisted the urge to touch it. If it had belonged to the Egyptian Queen, he wanted nothing to do with it. No telling what kind of whacked spell the thing carried. Unknown Egyptian magic. He shivered at the thought.

His gaze fell to the carved chest. The toy box, he presumed, even though the thing was more the size of a coffin. He glanced over his shoulder to verify Nell was still sleeping before slowly lifting the lid. His shoulders tensed as the hinges squeaked. Standing stock still, he listened. The sheets rustled. He looked over his shoulder once more to find she had turned slightly toward him. Her face was relaxed, her breathing even. Trent let out the breath he'd been holding as the lid continued its upward journey.

Three feet wide, two feet deep and at least eight feet long, the chest was layered with shelves, trays and nooks. Each item inside was meticulously arranged and displayed for the greatest ease of retrieval.

Trent couldn't decide where to look first. There was so much of…everything.

The dildos and vibrators he easily recognized. On other shelves were assortments of cock rings, feathers, floggers and some clamps—he wasn't sure he wanted to know where the latter were intended to be attached. He shook his head, unable to stop the images of the Halfling bound and blindfolded, her body stretched before him, back arched, breasts pushed upward, begging for his attention. He attempted to arrange his cock so the thing wasn't uncomfortably pressed against denim, but after adjusting twice he found no such position.

The buff leather caught his attention but the gleaming gold buckles held it. Trent tightened his fist to prevent himself from picking them up. He knew he shouldn't. He should shut the lid and go. He'd fantasized about her enough over the years; seeing all this wasn't helping his overactive imagination.

Reaching in, he ignored his own internal warnings.

With slightly trembling fingers, he lifted the cuff set out of the chest. The supple leather was oiled to perfection, the bindings polished and shining. It was a set of four, two slightly larger for her ankles.

That did it—completed his perfect erotic vision of the Halfling. No simple handcuffs would do for Nell. Nope. Perfect, high-grade, calf-hide-covered restraints, with gold buckles and big D loops for attaching them to most anything.

Trent's knees felt a little weak. He had to go. Now. He placed the bindings back in their nook and shut the lid to the chest. He turned without looking back at Nell. He couldn't. Not now.

* * * * *

It had been almost a week since Nell had watched Trent's face as he'd so reverently held up the cuffs. She shouldn't have spied on him, but he was looking through her box. Pandora's Box, as she called it.

Now she had the plan she needed.

When Trent left her room, she'd seen the strain in the line of his jaw, the tension in his muscles, how his fists were squeezed tight. She'd given it a week to let that tension boil, to let his fantasies fester. The night of the attack, Trent Nicholas gave away what she'd suspected for years. He wanted her as much as she wanted him. He held back, but he wanted. She didn't know exactly why he'd denied their pleasure for so long. The line he'd given her when they were younger was crap. It didn't matter that she was a Halfling; his pack was more open-minded than that and he'd known it even back then.

Yep. His resistance to her in the past had been veiled with empty excuses. There was something else, something the Prime was afraid to face. His self-denial went much deeper than his arrogantly flippant excuses—and self-denial it was. She'd seen it in his sour expressions and his hasty retreats.

For years she'd blamed herself. No more. Tonight she would push him. Tonight she'd get past that hot, sexy, gruff, arrogant exterior.

Nell looked up through the trees and waited as the moon started its nightly journey across the sky. Tonight, the moon would be full.

* * * * *

Trent checked the caller ID on his cell phone. Nell. He'd gotten some info on the case and needed to ask her some questions anyway. There were really no more excuses to put it off. He leaned against his car. "Nicholas."

He heard hissing, a rustle of what sounded like feet shuffling through dried leaves and then a grunt.

"Nell?"

More noise he couldn't identify, another grunt—and the distinct gurgling sound a person made when being choked.

"Nell!"

A loud thunk, a scream and louder crackling...

Followed by silence.

He was pacing now, staring blankly at the screen on his cell. *Dropped call*, it reported. Reception around these parts was always crap and calls often dropped, especially higher in the mountains. He hit the callback button. Busy.

How the fuck was he supposed to find her?

His pulse was racing, his palms sweating. He'd gotten a tip about an errant Sorcerer nosing around the area, asking questions. Had this character gotten to Nell before Trent could make his way back to her place? Someone should be watching her...

Guilt washed over him. Had he let her down? After all these years, had he truly missed his chance?

The phone rang again.

"Nell?"

Her voice was raspy. He heard the strain it took to utter the words. His fist hit the hood of his car hard enough to leave a dent. "Den...park..." The hissing overrode the next couple of words.

The plastic of his small cell phone cracked under the pressure of his grip. "Nell. Where. Are. You?"

"...the west." Her voice broke through the static before the line went dead again. He hit the callback button and got another busy signal.

The west entrance to Denning Park made sense. That part of the park butted up against Nell's land. He gritted his teeth as he slammed himself behind the wheel of his car, figuring he was about eight minutes away.

* * * * *

Nell left her cell phone, open and turned off, on the ground by a trail leading to the playground then tucked the small sheet of cellophane she'd used to create static into a pocket of her backpack. She broke several branches along the way, making sure her scent was left on the foliage. A Chihuahua could follow her trail. Trent Nicholas, supernatural super cop, would be on her in no time. Nell paused at the opening to the playground to look back over her shoulder. All was set. All she had to do was wait for a frantic Werewolf to show up—and then blow up.

She didn't wait long. He blasted through the trees without much noise. Nell managed to feign surprise at his arrival. Sitting back, resting on her elbows atop a picnic table, her knees slightly spread and her feet on the bench, she smiled at the disarray of his hair and clothing. He looked as though he'd run a mile. Well, technically he almost had. The trail that led to the playground was about that long. He stood still, staring at her with all the anger she knew was just about to bust through his tough-guy veneer.

"You're fine," he huffed.

"Why thank you, Trent." She sat up. He took two measured steps forward. Nell was sure he wanted to rush her and shake her. "You look a little rattled, sweets. What's wrong?"

He tossed her phone onto the table next to her. "You dropped this." He took his time looking her up and down. His gaze stirred her need more than she had anticipated. It was key she keep her cool for a little longer. His fists were balled tight against his thighs and she could see his pulse racing under the tanned skin of his neck. She swallowed her own racing desire and stood on the bench, knowing that the tight, white t-shirt and snug cut-off shorts were giving him a very good idea of her intentions.

"Oh, thanks." She took a step along the bench, *accidentally* kicking over the backpack lying next to her feet. The buff leather cuffs tumbled out. She never took her eyes off his as he watched them roll to the ground. His pupils narrowed, she heard the sharp intake of air followed by a guttural growl that made her tremble.

She looked up over his shoulder. The moon had made its way over the tree line. She smiled at the silver smudge among the hazy overcast of late-summer heat.

"You're flirting with the moon, little one." His voice was heavy, his body rigid, his eyes brighter and fixed on hers. "But you know that don't you?"

She turned away and started to pace the other direction, walking the bench like a balance beam, holding her arms out. She made it to the end and looked back at him over her shoulder. "You'd be amazed at what I know now, Trent." With that, she winked. She saw his eyes widen.

This was it. If he chased, he was hers. She needed to push his wolf and this was her chance. She'd spurred his protective nature with the phone call, the cuffs tempted the man—all she needed now was his wolf.

She jumped to the ground. Her hiking boots made a thud that echoed in the night as she landed in a slight crouch to suggest her intention to run. She met his gaze once more and his nostrils flared, his eyes darting to the path on her right and back to her face, an acknowledgment of her intentions.

He'd catch her. She had no doubt. What she needed was time to evade, to stir the wolf beyond Trent's control. He opened his mouth to speak but Nell didn't give him the chance to argue. She darted off toward the woods, pushing her legs hard to move, to run as fast as she could without calling her own Demon forward. Within fifty yards she felt his presence behind her. It wouldn't be long. She hoped it was enough as she gave her last effort to sidestep him by turning sharply around a tree.

His moves were fast and sure in the forest and he met her from the opposite side of the same tree. He bent forward, crashing into her, collapsing her over his shoulder with the impact. He straightened and started walking back to the playground.

She tried to lift herself up but he bounced her to adjust his hold, making Nell flop down, her breasts pressed into his back. She decided to appreciate the muscles moving under his shirt, the heat that emanated from his back, and hold his sides with her hands. This was an E-ticket ride and she wanted to remember every detail. She'd waited a very long time for Trent Nicholas.

He put her down on the bench, taking her hands in one of his as he reached for the cuffs and the backpack. He knelt in front of her, his eyes not making contact with hers as he worked to reverently wrap the supple leather around first one wrist then the other, latching the buckles together. Nell held her breath, her heart pounding from the run, brain swimming with the possibilities that lay before them. She wanted to say something, to get him to look at her, but she dared not break the moment.

After rummaging through the bag and removing a length of rope, he tossed the pack unceremoniously aside. He stood, finally making eye contact, his steely gaze stern and unwavering. Nell started to squirm. The heat in that gaze could set fire to the picnic table. Years of pent-up desires were bubbling to the surface. She wanted, *badly*. His stare said she wasn't alone, and now there was nothing between them but his reluctance. And, from the twitch of his lip, that reluctance was long gone as well.

She closed her eyes to steady her nerves, to drag in a breath and give herself a quick reality check. Before her breath was complete he lifted her roughly to her feet. Her eyes flew open. Trent backed her to the sturdy, nearby swing set and tossed the rope over the top beam. She glanced from his ice-blue eyes to the rope above her head, heart skipping a beat and her pussy throbbing in anticipation of his dominance. She had placed her bet on the right number. Submitting would push Trent Nicholas over the edge and into her arms. Well, right this minute her arms were being tightly strung over her head, but she smiled at her own cleverness.

After checking the knot of the rope that held Nell on her tiptoes, Trent grabbed her chin and tilted her head up. He was a good six inches taller than she. He leaned in and brushed his cheek against hers. She could feel his intake of breath against her skin. "Is this what you wanted, Nell?"

His sleek black hair was tousled, leaving a thick lock to fall into his eyes. Nell whimpered at the deep, hoarse and outrageously sexy tone his voice had taken on. He dug his fingers into her hair and looked into her eyes. "Are you sure you're ready for what moon lust brings?" His nostrils flared as she nodded her head. He held her gaze as he pulled her head farther back before leaning in to nuzzle his face between her breasts.

Apparently unhappy with the fabric between them, he used his pocketknife to cut off her t-shirt. She wore nothing underneath. Cicadas serenaded in the heat of the mountain evening. Heaven. It was all Nell's idea of heaven.

"Yes, Trenton. Yes." Nell's words were little more than a whisper.

Trent's head jerked up and he stepped away as if she'd slapped him.

"Trent?"

He backed away about ten feet and stopped, shoved a shaking hand through his hair before abruptly turning and walking toward the trail.

"Trenton Nicholas, you are *not* going to leave me like this!" She had meant it to be a very firm command, but as his form disappeared into the tree line, her tone changed to that of an uneasy question. "Trent?" Her arousal transformed to an immediate frustration born of an acute understanding of her situation. She was half-naked, cuffed and hanging from a swing set in a national forest. Great.

She looked around, listened for him to come back, but all she heard was the diminishing sound of his pine-straw-muffled steps. "Damn it. *Damn it.* Motherfuc— Damn it." She struggled against the bindings and against her Demon change. That's all she needed.

She concentrated and tried to focus her energy toward the rope holding her up on her toes. The muscles in her thighs and calves were starting to scream. She shifted uneasily from one leg to the other, finding no relief to the burning, as she used her power to try to break the rope.

Nell concentrated hard and sent a small surge of power toward her wrists. She grumbled as the rope turned black in reaction to her magic, but didn't break or even fray. Her wrists, on the other hand, felt like she'd banged them with a hammer.

"Great plan, Nell! Push his wolf…yeah, that was just brilliant. Let's face it, girl. The man does *not* want you." She tried to adjust again. Giving up on being comfortable, Nell let herself sink into the bindings, stretching her arms for a moment instead of her legs.

No. She was almost positive Trent wanted her as badly as she wanted him. Either way, she had to get out of this predicament before she could decide if it was *Trent* she'd misjudged, or her plan.

Her shaky Demon power of telekinesis just wasn't well directed enough to unbuckle the cuffs or untie or destroy the rope. She could try something less intricate, like breaking the top beam of the swing, but she couldn't get out of the way of the bulky timber if she did manage to make it fall. More than likely she would make it explode and the heavy beam would come crashing on her head, catching her hair on fire.

She looked down over her exposed breasts. "Just great, Nell. What if whoever tried to off you the other night is lurking around here?" She shook her head.

After the attack, Nell had been badgered into taking turns staying at her sisters' and Mi-Ma's houses all week. It'd taken forever to convince Sonja and Trina that she needed some time alone. Now she was alone all right. At least they would miss her in a little while and come looking for her. Maybe Sonja would have a vision of her stupid ass tied up in the playground.

Nell jumped a she felt the presence of something behind her.

"Would serve you right." Trent's voice was stern in her ear. Adrenaline poured through her body as Trent grabbed her hair from behind and bent her head back. "Don't say anything, Demon. You understand me?"

Nell nodded. She had no intention of speaking and ruining anything. He pulled her against his chest and Nell realized he had shed his shirt. The heat of his body, the strength of his grip and the rough hairs on his chest all strummed at her nerves and heated her to boiling.

Using his free hand, he traced a line up her side, not being gentle. His touch was purposeful, his nails slightly scratching their way over each of her ribs. With her head tilted back, she could see his face as he watched the trail his fingers made over her skin. He was savoring the tiny reactions her muscles made to his rough touch, the goose bumps left behind. When the trail reached the base of her breast, he paused, tilting his head as if to consider his path. Nell held her breath as his hand flattened and his palm closed over her flesh. He squeezed and she felt her legs tremble from the pleasure of his touch and the strain of being on her toes for so long.

Trent grunted and stopped the attention he was paying her breast. She tightened her muscles as he dug in his pocket and Nell heard the snap of the pocketknife again. He moved around her, working the knife expertly, and her shorts were shredded as fast as the t-shirt had been, leaving her hanging naked and facing his intense gaze.

He swung one of the swings over the upper beam twice, studied the height for a moment then reached over and cut the rope that had been holding Nell to the beam. Trent took no time to soothe her weak and tingling arms before he bent her forward over the swing, resting her stomach on the thick rubber seat. With her hands still bound together, Nell tried to gain some sense of balance but she couldn't find anything to hold on to. Her toes barely touched the ground, just as they had when she was upright. The position left her completely vulnerable, forced to let her body fall forward and do the best she could to balance with the toes of her boots and the swing seat.

Trent held her hips as he lowered himself to a kneeling position behind her. With her head hanging forward, she could see his bent knees between her legs. He roughly pulled her cheeks apart and leaned in to run his pointed tongue from her throbbing clit to her ass and back with little gentleness.

Nell gasped at the intensity of the unexpected sensation. The rough treatment of her ass checks was contradictory to the silky touch of his tongue as he lingered over her clit, teasing her until her legs trembled, leaving only her weight and Trent's hands holding her in the seat. With tightly closed eyes, Nell concentrated on the wind howling through the tops of the pines, the smell of a distant campfire mixed with that of the damp, mossy ground and the feel of Trent's skin against hers. She wanted to memorize the moment Trent Nicholas gave in, the moment *she* gave in.

She felt him stand and heard the unmistakable sound of a zipper. She tried to look back but he grasped her shoulders, pushing her down, holding her in place. Leaning forward, he wrapped his bigger body over hers, nuzzled his face in the back of her hair—and gave a small growl as he buried himself balls-deep into her dripping pussy.

"Trent!" Nell almost squealed.

He pushed her forward, using the swing to move her body away from his, until just the tip of his cock was inside her. He was so hard and she could feel the ridge of his head pulling against her opening, then he yanked her back, reseating himself forcefully and wrenching a gasping moan from Nell.

"Hush, baby." Again he withdrew, pushing her forward before pulling her back, grunting and driving his cock into her depths.

Arms dangling and unable to do more than hold her head up, Nell let herself experience complete surrender to Trent Nicholas. She was, for the moment anyway, his, completely and without question. His to do with as he pleased, and it was the most liberating feeling she had ever known. She tightened the muscles gripping his cock, to let him know she could still add to his pleasure, to show him she wanted this and would contribute to her surrender. He gripped her hips hard, let out a roaring growl and increased his speed. With each thrust of his cock Nell grunted uncontrollably, which seemed to become more guttural and animalistic as his arousal, and his pace, increased.

Her orgasm built slowly, despite the grueling pace the Were had set. With each thrust he brought her closer. She tightened her muscles again to get the most from his efforts — and it hit. She tried to gain some footing to push back and hold him steady as she came.

He stopped, holding her tight against his hips, buried deep. Trent let out a throaty moan as her pussy fluttered around his cock. "Nell, baby. Yes. Fuck. That's good."

He held her against him, letting her savor her explosion for only a moment before he pulled out then grasped her by the shoulders, pulled her upright and turned her to face him. "So fucking sexy." He kissed her hungrily, biting at her lips until she opened them. Nell was weak from her orgasm and overwhelmed by the feeling of being so needed. And he *did* need her. He may never admit it openly, but she felt it in every want-filled, hungry touch out here under the moon.

His free hand moved up her back, pulling her against his body, and she could feel his jeans still at his knees. Trent's tongue invaded her mouth, leaving no doubt that this man did everything with wicked intent. There would be precious few times the wolf was soft and sappy. No, her wolf was wild and untamed and that's exactly what had always attracted her. He was man enough to match her, man enough to best her on occasion, and man enough to meet her strong Demon needs.

Trent maneuvered them until he was sitting in the other swing, kicking off his jeans and boots in the process. He lifted Nell and sat her astride his lap, thighs between the chains and his waist. She watched silently as he unhooked the clips that bound her cuffs together and placed her hands on the chains. His gaze lingered over her wet and swollen pussy before moving up her body. He leaned in and took a nipple in his teeth, biting with just the right amount of force to make Nell tighten her grip on the chains and let her head fall back. The movement pushed her wet pussy against his still-hard cock. He released his tight bite on her nipple and teased the lingering sting with little flicks of his tongue.

Nell was whimpering, wondering how long she could hold the chains and not grab his head and pull him closer, begging for more, more of his tongue, more of his attention. He moved to her other breast and repeated the torture, biting, teasing. She was writhing on his lap, pleading with louder and louder moans.

Had this been any other man she would have grabbed him, steered the situation to her needs, her wants, and then likely felt empty and unsatisfied even after her completion. But this wasn't any other man.

When Nell was sure she could take no more of his teasing torment, Trent stopped and ran his hands over her back and kissed his way up to her ear. "What do you want, baby?"

"You."

"More specific, little Demon." He bit her neck, causing her head to fall back again, giving her the perfect view of the full moon.

"Fuck me, Prime."

He chuckled and lifted her ass just enough to set her back on his cock. He lowered her slowly, giving her a chance to savor the feel of him stretching her. "I think," he said as he leaned back, moving the swing forward, "we'll do some easy swinging." He shifted again and the swing changed direction.

As Nell leaned back, the motion tilted her hips, opening her for even greater penetration. When the swing changed direction again and her body leaned forward, she squeezed her thighs, lifting her hips just slightly and giving him a slight withdrawal, not much, just a little. They rocked back and forth. As momentum swung them forward, her body shifted toward his, his cock thrusting deep inside her. Nell pressed herself down on him fully, pushing her hips into him. As the momentum stopped at the back end of the swing's arch, Nell leaned her upper body back. His cock thrust inside her farther. She moaned.

The gentle back-and-forth motion and the intense way the Were watched her body move as she pumped them back and forth, moving the swing in a steady motion, driving him in and out of her, was drawing another raging orgasm to the surface. His face no longer hid his emotions. The tight expression he usually wore was replaced by a look of serenity and acceptance. Nell leaned back farther, taking them higher. She was getting close, and if the tightening of his jaw was any indicator, he was as well.

She clenched her legs around his sides, hooking her feet behind his back. The swing kept moving but lost its momentum as she ground down onto his engorged cock. Trent gripped her hips. "That's it, Nell. Come for me, baby."

She tossed her head back again, looking for the moon as he howled and drove into her one last time, pushing them both over the edge and into bliss. Nell shouted his name to the moon as her orgasm rocked her.

Chapter Four

ℰᗏ

Trent held the trembling Halfling in his arms. She fit there, with her head tucked under his chin, her wrists still wrapped in the cuffs and resting on his chest. He replayed the entire scene in his head. He'd been rougher with her than he had intended. Hell, when he turned around to come back and check on her, he had just intended to watch over her until she figured a way out of the cuffs. He'd intended to leave Nell Ambercroft alone. But as he watched her struggle with the bindings, the way her body moved, and as he smelled the musky scent of her arousal, the forceful yearning of his wolf waylaid those intentions. He could no longer resist the woman who had tempted him for so long and he'd let the animal take her.

Nell moaned and readjusted slightly, his soft cock sliding out of her, falling wet and warm between his thighs, pulling a pouting whimper and little moan from her. From the limpness of her body, he didn't think she wanted to move. He wanted to enjoy the feel of her against his chest for as long as possible, so he held her, not letting her move from his lap.

A long, low howl in the distance reminded him of their surroundings. A chorus of other Weres answered the first and their songs echoed across the mountain. Trent felt his wolf stretch and stir, but it was happily sated. Probably more sated than it had been in years. No urge to change and no restless cravings goading him to hunt under the moon this night. The full moon was always host to several ceremonies and rituals in the area. Trent was now glad he'd made no commitments to appear at any of them.

He pushed off, swinging them slightly as he trailed his fingers up and down her spine, enjoying the feel of each of the delicate bones, the taut muscles and the silky skin that covered them.

"Halfling," he whispered to the top of her golden hair. Another set of baying howls filled the humid night air. "We should get you covered up before we have company."

"Um hm." She lifted her head and gave him a lazy smile. "My being naked didn't bother you a bit a few minutes ago."

Unable to resist, Trent kissed her long and softly, feeling the warmth of her lips, teasing the tip of her tongue with his. This pleasant, replete female would soon be back to her loud, bossy self. He wanted to savor her this way for just a minute more, remember her this way—not angry, as she would be when he parted ways with her. She tasted of everything forbidden to him and it was starting to hurt. He should have kept going, gotten in his car and left her hanging from the swing. It might have been safer for her that way.

Breaking the kiss, he held her shoulders and looked her in the eye. He would not take the coward's way out of this. "You're right, but there are others gathering up here tonight. We won't be alone for long. You need to get home and I have work to do."

"You're not coming with me?"

"No. I told you before. I've tried to avoid this. To avoid using you."

She sat up in his lap, grinding her still moist, warm pussy against him. Trent took in a raspy breath as the realization crossed her face. He needed to get his point across. She had to know he couldn't start a relationship. He braced himself for her anger, wishing he had another option.

"Use me?" she asked.

"Nell. You don't understand." Her struggle to extract herself from his lap cut off his feeble explanation. She was trying to pull her legs from around his hips but was hampered by the chains. She fell backward, cursing. It gave him a wonderful view, since her legs were still straddling him.

Gripping her hips, he lifted her curvy form and set her on the ground before him. She was so beautiful, so strong and so perfect for him in every way. If only he were able to be the man she needed.

"You rotten dog!" She put her hands on her naked hips and her breasts jiggled. Trent tried to concentrate on her face but her nipples were calling to him. He'd taken her so fast and rough that he'd not had time to enjoy her shapely body. She kept right on talking. "What is it, Trent? I just proved I could take whatever you and your wolf can dish out. I'm not as fragile as I look. You want me. I bet if you look inside that mangy chest of yours and find what was once something close to a heart, you'd see that you love me. Why, Trent? Why?"

"Nell. It's not you."

"Damn straight it's not me. I proved to you what I've always known. Your animal side has never scared me, wolf-boy. So what is it?"

He didn't answer.

She stomped back to the table and grabbed her backpack. Trent took the opportunity to slide his pants and boots on as she pulled out a clean set of shorts and a tank top. "All these years, every time we've seen one another, I could see your feelings written all over your face. And Mi-ma tells me you've kept up with me, even checked on me more often than necessary." She yanked the top over her head.

She didn't stop glaring at him as she stepped into her shorts, not until her booted foot caught and made her stumble. Trent tried to reach out to catch her but she had already started to use her Demon magic to catch her fall, creating a magical buffer between herself and the ground. Trent broke the spell as he moved closer, causing them both to fall. Their eyes met. Hers were filled with anger and hurt. It showed in the depths of those golden brown irises.

He inwardly cringed. He hated hurting her more than anything. She yanked herself up, adjusted her shorts and zipped them.

"Oh no you don't. Don't you pity me, Prime. This is *your* loss." She unbuckled the gold bindings on one of the cuffs. "I waited. I gave you room to sow your wild oats." She threw the cuff into his lap. "I let you do the brooding loner thing." She released the second cuff and tossed it. The buff leather cuff landed perfectly next to the first on his thighs. "This was it, Trent. I'm done. We've shared blood. We're all but mated as it is. Whatever it is that's holding you back, share it with me and we'll work through it together." She slung the pack over her shoulder and looked down at him.

Trent felt his insides churn. The wolf was up and pacing, uneasy and growling in his mind. He wanted to tell her. He really did. But how did you tell the woman you've always loved that you're afraid? Afraid you'll kill her in a fit of groundless jealousy or unrestrained anger? He looked to his feet, trying to find the strength to admit his weakness. His feet didn't possess the ability to assist him.

Nell stood quietly looking down at him, waiting for an answer, waiting for Trent to share his thoughts for several excruciatingly long minutes, but he kept his silence.

"I don't even deserve a response from you? I mean that little?" she asked quietly.

She waited again for an answer. He had none.

"Fine. I'll not wait for you anymore, Trent Nicholas." Her voice cracked slightly. She turned and started up the path that led toward her house without a backward glance.

Trent's gaze dropped to the supple leather cuffs in his lap and he wondered how he would ever get past the feeling of her skin on his fingers. Would he sleep again without dreaming of the way she had joyfully encouraged his dominant urges, or how much it had turned her on to do so?

Would he ever hear the wind and not hear the breathless moans she made when she came apart as she rode him?

A long, lonely howl sang through the silence of the night. He understood the emptiness in the sound as it echoed through the mountain air, making his wolf stretch and pace.

He still had business to attend to. The wolf would have to wait this time.

Chapter Five

౭౦

"Fucking Demons," Trent muttered before turning back to an old Demon who was sucking on an ugly tattoo plastered across the hip of a prostitute. The pert brunette was naked and spread out over the trunk lid of a crappy old Chrysler. The Demon had done little to acknowledging the Prime's questions. "Carson, just tell me before I decide you're violating some Council tenet."

The Demon pulled himself away from the hooker, making her moan in objection. "Easy, bitch. I'm paying by the hour." His appearance shifted. The change was fast and subtle, but Trent saw a ripple of transformation. Most likely a side effect of the sexual excitement Carson was fighting to stem in order to speak.

"You know, Prime, this had best be important. I'm as liable to fuck you as her in this state."

Trent snorted. "Try." The hooker giggled. The Demon continued to stroke her even with his attention turned to the Were. Trent noticed her tight body and young features did nothing for him. Not that he was one for hookers anyway, but the female should at least pique his interest. Full moon, his wolf should be stirring, ready to go at anything with a pussy. The sight of the girl naked and splayed over the car only made him wonder what Nell would look like bent over the back of his Mustang, her legs spread wide, looking over her shoulder at him.

He huffed and looked the Demon in the eye. "Have you heard of any new masters in the area? Any new faces at all?" This was Small Town, Nowhere, tucked high in the mountains. If there was a new Sorcerer around, the low-level Demons always knew. The rats were usually recruited to do the grunt work uppity masters didn't want to dirty their hands with — like maiming a Halfling.

Carson hesitated in his ministrations of the female for a split second, the move as slight as the ripple of a change earlier, but Trent noticed. "No, man." Carson turned back and leaned over the girl's breasts, taking one in his mouth.

"Carson. I'm asking one more time. I smelled blood magic. On a dead human. *Serious* blood magic. That means a master Sorcerer is being very naughty. You don't want to be a party to that sort of violation. The Council — "

Carson pulled his lips away from the girl's tit with a pop. "Council? I'd rather face the Council than the problems *you're* looking for, man. But you cut me some slack once, so I'll tell you something you can use." He looked around. The hooker whined again, so Carson started rubbing her clit to shut her up. "You don't need no master for blood magic. You only need a pissant Sorcerer and a good *spell* from a master for that."

"Fine. So what pissant has come to town?"

Carson smirked. "After your girl, ain't he?"

Trent roared as he lunged. He plowed into Carson, taking them both to the ground. The hooker squealed and rolled off the hood, landing in a pile on the far side of the rusty, old car. Trent let his snout lengthen as he lightly sank his teeth into the Demon's exposed throat. No matter what form the Demon chose for this fight, Trent now had the advantage.

Carson tried to still his body. "Okay, man. You got me."

Trent loosened his bite enough to get out a garbled word. "Talk."

"A skank Sorcerer I hadn't seen in forty years showed up last week. Says he's been looking for a chick from his past. Says he wants to *play* with her. I know who he's asking after and who she belongs to, dude. I swear. I didn't tell him shit. He must have found her some other way."

Trent's teeth tightened on Carson's neck. The hair on the back of Trent's neck was sprouting. He tasted Demon blood and sweat on his tongue. He tried to take deep, full breaths. The wolf was raging, pressing on his mind, stretching in his body. His fingers burned with the need to change, his nails already lengthening.

"Dude, I should have told you! But the guy's a bug. I didn't think he'd do her any harm, honest. I figured she'd kick his ass to another realm." Leathery-feeling, partially changed skin formed under Trent's teeth as Carson also tried for deep breaths, desperately trying to calm down. "Easy, man. Take a deep breath. Don't go full wolf and rip me apart, dude." Trent felt him shaking under his grip. "Think of the Council paperwork!"

Trent caught himself laughing. He released the Demon and rolled away and into a sitting position.

Carson propped himself on his elbow. "He didn't hurt your woman, did he?"

Trent spat. "She's not my woman."

The Demon relaxed onto his back as the hooker scrambled away from the car. "Whatever you tell yourself, man." He watched the frightened female as she made it to her own car. "That was a good lay too." He rubbed his head.

"Name, Carson." The night was wearing on him and the moon was still calling.

"Crey."

* * * * *

The backpack slid across the coffee table, taking out magazines and candles as it made its way to the floor in front of the couch. Nell kept moving toward the stairs, not caring to see the damage. "I'm done." Hot, angry tears trailed down her face.

She reached the base of the stairs—and froze, holding her breath, trying to squelch the tears and the pounding of her heart.

The tiny hairs on the back of her neck tingled.

Something was wrong.

She stood stock-still and listened to the house. The normal sounds of wind and old, creaking wood. Off in the distance she could hear the excited melody of wolf cries as they embraced the moon. She could see the back door and part of the kitchen at the end of the short hall that ran past the stairs. Her heart twisted again as she remembered Trent carrying her out that door, cradling her tenderly, but she stifled the emotion to concentrate on the more pressing feeling of dread.

She had to sniffle. Her nose was running. Damn that arrogant Were! She had put herself in danger because she was distracted by him again. She should have gone straight to Mima's. She just needed to find her car keys and then she'd be out of there…

No. This was *her* house. Her father's house. She'd be damned if she'd let anyone scare her away.

Nell glanced around her immediate area. Nothing seemed out of place, so she turned quietly to face the living room. The darkness did little to hide anything. Her night vision had been acclimated by the long walk through the forest, and was excellent regardless. She listened once more. Nothing.

She took a step toward the kitchen and her hair tickled again. The source of her unease was in that direction. Nell's instincts had gotten her through many a bad situation and she trusted them without fail. Well, except for where that stupid, stubborn wolf was concerned.

A branch, swaying in the breeze, tapped on the window in the dining room. Nell took another step. She felt as if her heart was pounding loud enough to give her position away. She drew in on herself, felt her shift coming. She fought it. She needed her intellect at the moment. In her shifted form, she was all primal urge. If she were a full Demon, like her father and Mi-ma, her shifted form would be significantly bigger, stronger and still as sentient. Her Halfling Demon form made her slightly bigger and a little stronger, but in it, she tended toward the fight-or-flight response; she felt and reacted. She needed to think right this minute.

Nell took a deep, steadying breath and slid around the wall that blocked most of the kitchen from view. Only shadows danced in the room. That left the basement. She shivered. She hated the basement in broad daylight. Going down there while she had this spooky feeling did *not* make her happy.

She moved as quietly as she could back to the living room and rummaged through her backpack. Shit. She'd left her cell phone on the picnic table in the park. And since moving back home, she'd not bothered to hook up the phone. She had her cell. What did she need a landline for? Now she really needed the Prime and she'd left herself with no way to reach him. *Great plan, Nelly.*

Nell cautiously crept back to the kitchen, casting a wistfully longing glance at the old rotary phone on the wall, its cord impossibly tangled. Her pistol lay in a cabinet drawer directly beneath the useless phone. She cringed when the wood, swollen with age, released a brief, high-pitched squeal as she opened the drawer.

The door to the basement stood ajar at the back of the kitchen. That wasn't unusual. She always left the door cracked. It was a constant ritual for her, looking down those rickety stairs first thing every morning, even before brewing coffee. Not that anything had ever greeted her from the landing, but…just in case. Call it crazy superstition but various items from her dad's travels were down there and the room had its own peculiar vibration that gave her the jeebies. No telling what batshit-crazy stuff was hidden away in those boxes — and no way was she closing the door on it. If something decided to manifest down there, she wanted to see it coming.

At the moment the basement looked like a dark abyss. Like a cop on television, she held the gun out, ready to aim and fire as she moved.

She closed her eyes and steeled her nerves. She put her foot on the first step, listening, knowing that every time she watched a scary movie she cursed the chicks who went into scary, dark basements.

Nell had always thought she would be smarter than that. Apparently not. This was no movie and she knew exactly what evils lurked in the dark. To some, she would *be* that evil. But someone—or *something*—was down there and she wanted this to end. She was tired of sleeping on her sisters' couches. She let her fear push her to the point of partially shifting. Her bones started to lengthen, grinding at the joints. Her teeth scraped together as they dropped, giving her small, pointy fangs.

She felt her Demon presence very close to the surface and used that energy to feel for any sign of life force in the basement. She was sure she would have to battle for her life again. More dead things in the house she would have to deal with. Hopefully she wouldn't be one of them.

Nell rushed down to the basement, half-shifted, gun pointed into the darkness. At the bottom of the stairs she was swarmed by shadow. It moved; she felt the touch of it. She let her shift complete, her size increasing only minimally, her skin shimmering into a tough-scaled hide, her eyesight sharpening.

She spun as the shadow engulfed her. Nell fired. She reached out with her telekinesis as well and thrust with her Demon power, but even with her improved night vision she couldn't find the source of the shadow to attempt to focus on it. The power bounced around the stone walls of the basement. She couldn't stop the force once she let it go. It reverberated, knocking over a table. The blast hit her as well. She stumbled backward and tripped over some displaced objects that once lived neatly on shelves.

The shadow felt thick and was, amazingly, attacking from all around her. Her heart beat faster. Through the engulfing shadow she thought she saw a darker shape moving swiftly toward her.

She concentrated through her fear, fought the flight instinct and raised the gun. She squeezed the trigger again.

A strange, deafening shriek echoed off the cinderblock basement walls...

Then all got quiet for a moment.

She looked up. The shadow was still moving around her and she held her breath, unable to fight it in any other way. How do you stop a shadow? She resigned herself to waiting for an actual attack. She was weakened by such a large surge of magic. She wasn't able to call on her telekinesis as much as she liked, and after the emotional night and a panicked burst of energy that big, she was toast.

Her breathing calmed. She held the gun pointed at the far wall as the shadow began to take on a more physical presence. It wasn't a shadow after all. It was a bunch of life forces, flying, flitting and finally starting to settle around the room.

Shaking her head as she turned on the light, Nell realized she had fired a gun—and then sent a huge blast of her power—at a bunch of moths. Many of them were still flitting, a few toward the blaring light fixture, others haphazardly in reaction to her movements, but the majority of them were alighting to a particular place. Past the overturned table, close to the far wall, was a box on its side, spilled open, papers and stones strewn across the floor. It was a box of research papers. She recognized the writing on one of the scattered documents. The moths were all heading toward the contents of the box.

The creatures stirred again as she moved through them. The design on the moths seemed familiar, as if she should recognize the significance of the blue and silver markings on their wings. But then, everything meant *something*. Surely a basement full of six-inch black moths was a harbinger. As if she needed this day to get any more stressful.

The winged insects were clamoring over the box, hundreds of the black, blue and silver beasts clung to the cardboard, the pages and the stones. Nell glanced at the lone window. Broken. She turned back to the stairs, still pointing the gun, ready to fire, and allowed her body to gently shift back to her human form. The golden, glowing shadow of the Dragon under her skin melted back to soft, tanned human flesh. She felt more comfortable in this body, even if it was far more vulnerable

A trail of blood led up the stairs. She'd hit someone or something. She followed the trail through the kitchen and out onto the deck. Whatever she'd shot, it was gone now. She locked the door as she went back in.

Back in the basement she settled her attention on the scattered papers. Her father's shakily printed words covered the pages. His notes from Scotland. His last excursion.

The shipping labels and stickers had kept Nell away from these particular boxes. She wasn't ready to go through the last of his work.

Personal effects – Gregor Ambercroft.

Isle of Skye. Scotland.

Handle with care.

One of the moths fluttered to her, landing on her arm. Tiny legs gripping the faint hair made her shiver. She scanned the depths of the shelves in the basement one more time. She was alone. Alone with a thousand moths and a mystery.

The moth opened and closed its wings in a slow, steady, hypnotic rhythm. The markings on it were vibrant in the harsh light of the bare bulb. Nell reached down and righted the overturned table, then tried to get the moth to move off her arm. The thing clung stubbornly to its spot.

Another joined the first, and then another. If she'd been afraid of insects this would be a very trying event. "All right, kids, this isn't going to work." She shooed them as she tried to gather the contents of the spilled box onto the table. "What brought you all here this evening?"

Two other boxes had landed on their sides on the floor, still concealing their contents behind generous amounts of shipping tape. Somebody had wanted these things sealed tight. But this one had opened and scattered easily.

The notes were normal descriptions of a cave system, the drawings mundane and scientific. On most pages, anyway. She found several yellow legal pad pages stapled together, also with her father's handwriting, that didn't match the rest of the research notes. The print on these pages was from edge to edge and top to bottom, no margins and very few spaces. It was crowded and messy. Not that his usual print wasn't hard enough to decipher, but this was almost illegible.

Nell gathered the remaining spilled papers, scanning the notes, articles and newspaper clippings. All of them on the Isle of Skye caves. She emptied the box, flipping through the documents. Nothing else seemed out of the ordinary. Other than the freaking moths. Nothing looked worthy of stealing, worthy of an attack. She picked up the box...

And the moths converged, fluttering and landing on her head, her shoulders, on the box.

She dropped the box to the table and waved her hands wildly over her head in a vain attempt to scatter the moths. They clung, walking and fluttering their wings over her body and hair. More and more of them took to the air to swarm her. Nell stepped away from the table and tried to shake them off. Some fell away but took no time in returning.

"I don't want to hurt any of you, but you're starting to freak me out." Her Demon power would do little good in this situation. She was good for flinging dildos, but intricate work to safely remove confused moths was way out of her league. "Crap."

She hated to do it, but she brushed the few from her face and eyes. She felt their wings fold and bend as she did so and grimaced. She knew these things were somehow significant and wanted to do as little damage as possible. They weren't native to the area. Something brought them here.

A tiny spark of magic made Nell pause. She wasn't extremely sensitive to the magic of others, not like her sister Sonja was, but she knew blood magic when she felt it.

She froze, letting the moths continue their attempts to cover her body. She listened and tried to reach out again, to sense an intruder.

Nothing.

She raised a hand and scrunched her eyes enough to really study the creatures. She turned her hand palm up and two moved to cover her fingers and palm.

And she felt it.

In her fingers at first, then she opened herself to it fully. Tiny little sparks of magic were emanating from the moths.

"What *are* you?" she questioned as she inspected the insects. The winged harbingers remained silent. Mi-ma would know, and Nell was ready to get the heck out of the basement and the house. She glanced down to see several moths still lingered on the box itself, but only around the bottom. She lifted the box to see if there was anything unusual on the exterior to attract them. It was empty but still felt bulky, as though it were still stuffed full.

"Tricky." She turned it over and thumped the bottom. Solid. She looked around for something to break the tape. Moths fluttered and struggled to stay with her as she moved across the large room to a toolbox in the corner.

"You gals are going to have to hang on a little tighter." Nell slashed the tape with a box cutter from the toolbox and opened the bottom flaps to reveal a beautiful, dark panel of wood. She righted the box and cut the false bottom from the inside, the cardboard falling away to reveal what looked like an exotic wooden case. She pulled the rest of the cardboard away and was left holding what she strongly suspected was a colossal powder keg.

The dark-grained wood was the color of coffee beans and just as shiny, with veins of red streaked through it like thin streams of blood. At a foot square and about three inches deep, it felt much lighter than she would have thought something of its size should have been. It had no seams that she could see. It just looked like a solid chunk of wood, but she knew better.

This was getting more and more interesting.

The moths swarmed around the room in an attempt to get closer to her, closer to the box. She scooped up the stapled notes and headed up the stairs. "So this is what someone's after." She looked at the largest group of the moths that had gathered on her chest. "If you want me, you're going to have to keep up, ladies."

* * * * *

Trina screeched even before the door was fully opened. Nell's youngest sister backpedaled away from her as she stood in the doorway. Despite Nell's best efforts, many of the moths had managed to make it into the car and were stubbornly hanging on. Even open windows and broken speed limits couldn't suck the moths out of her life.

"Black Witch," Trina hissed and turned toward the kitchen. "Mi-ma! Nell's brought Black Witch moths into the house!"

Nell had suspected someone around here would know what the little buggers were. But she wasn't exactly happy about Trina's reaction or the tattletale tone in her voice. "Not a good omen, huh? Crap."

Mi-ma met Nell in the dining room. "One would think not, what with a name like Black Witch."

"I'm not exactly asking for their company." She looked back at the closed front door. "I suspect more will be showing up. You may want to close the windows." Nell pulled the papers and the box out of her backpack.

Mi-ma pulled a moth off Nell's head and inspected the wings. "Black Witch moths are known to be harbingers of death. Where did they find you?"

"The basement." Trina and Sonja joined them at the table after closing the windows and Nell quickly related the story. All three sisters looked to their grandmother for answers.

Mi-ma ran her hands over the box as if her fingers had x-ray vision and could see through the wood, unlocking all its mysteries. She set it on the table and tapped her round chin as one of the moths lighted on her fuzzy gray hair. "There's a blood-magic cult that mixes African Voodoo, animal sacrifices…" She hunched her shoulders and shivered. "This box feels dark like that. The moths would make sense if this is a Voodoo trinket."

"I don't like the sound of that," Trina said. "Did you get mixed up with a blood-magic cult when you were off gallivanting all over the world?"

Nell looked at Trina. Her bright blue eyes truly looked concerned. "Um, blood magic? Me? Right, Trina. I was traveling. I spent time in spas and four-star hotels. I wasn't off looking for trouble. No cults." She looked at Sonja. "Wouldn't your Spidey senses have told you if I was doing blood magic?"

Trina crossed her arms. "Vampire nests aren't exactly what I would consider spas."

Nell huffed. Sonja picked up the box and clutched it to her breast. Several of the moths fluttered toward her, making shadows dance over the table. "I don't like the energy this thing gives off at all. It's made *for* evil, *by* evil."

"Why would Dad have anything like that?" Trina looked to Mi-ma, who'd settled into the big chair at the end of the dark oak table. The same table Ambercrofts had sat around while discussing family issues, celebrating successes and sharing their lives for generations.

She let out a big breath. "Gregor was much like our Nell, always into something. You never knew *what* that boy was up to."

Nell smiled at the thought of anyone other than Mi-ma calling her father "boy". She went over and rubbed her grandmother's shoulders. Touching Mi-ma calmed her. "We need to get it open," Nell said as the moths returned. She brushed her forehead to encourage the creatures to remain out of her face.

Sonja put the ominous wooden box back on the table. They all contemplated the consequences of opening this particular package. "We need to call the Prime. *Twice* you've been attacked over this box." She picked up the notes and paged through them as she spoke

"No way, no how, am I dealing with that Prime ever again."

Mi-ma huffed. "I believe Sonja is right here, Nelly."

Nell grabbed the box off the table and walked it over to the kitchen counter. Turning it slowly under the brighter light in the kitchen, she examined it. "I think we should at least try to open it ourselves first. I don't need the Prime to figure this out." She retrieved a knife out of the dish rack and poked at the side.

"Nell!" Trina shrieked. "What the heck are you doing? What if it's spelled?"

Nell balanced the box on its side and poked the blade into another spot. "Haven't you noticed all the giant moths floating around me? You know, the harbinger-of-death bugs?" She banged the wooden box on the counter, scattering a couple of them. She inspected it for damage then scrunched up her face in frustration. "More like hexed, I suspect."

Trina walked up beside her. "You are so stubborn." She took the box and looked it over.

"No scorching, please," Nell said. Trina's Demon gift was rare and hard to manage. They were all a little unpredictable with their powers but Trina had to be the most careful. Fire starting was useful at times, backyard barbecues and lighting candles and such, but the rest of the time it was dangerous. Trina lived in a cinderblock house and still had problems when she got upset. She stayed away from people. That way, she prevented herself from singeing strangers with an absentminded hand gesture.

"Not funny." Trina brushed the top of the box with her fingertips. She returned to the dining room and handed it back to Mi-ma. "Feel the texture of the reddish grain. It's slightly raised."

Sonja looked at Nell over her glasses, dark hair falling into her eyes as she did so. "I think we need some reinforcements."

"No Prime," Nell insisted. "He won't know what the hell to do with it either. He'll just turn it over to the Council. They'll keep it for their own use. If it's worth killing over, it's bound to be valuable. I want to know what it is first."

Sonja sat. "I didn't think about that. You're right. We shouldn't show Trent. Heck, it's ours. It was in our basement. Why does he need to know anyway?"

Nell eyed her sister. That was quite the one-eighty. But then, Sonja had always lived here and routinely remained uninvolved. Happy in her little cottage tucked in the mountains. Happy to stay close to Mi-ma and family. Nell was pretty sure the thought of having to deal with the Council in any way frightened her little sister. It should. "Right. It's ours."

Unless someone else comes looking for it, Nell thought.

Chapter Six

ℬ

"The deadbeat hasn't paid me in two weeks. You pay his bill and you're in." The smelly, old clerk gave Trent a sideways grin accented with one gold tooth and two or three empty spaces where teeth may have once lived.

It was nearly two a.m. and he'd finally traced Crey to this slimy hotel. Maybe he'd get lucky and catch the Sorcerer asleep. He tossed a couple twenties on the counter. "I seem to be making regular contributions to your retirement, old man."

The clerk snickered, brushed his greasy gray hair out of his face and took a swig out of an unlabeled bottle. "Retirement. Sure." He tucked the bottle into his back pocket and fished a key out of a shoebox on the counter. "I'll be moving to Jamaica or someplace sunny, I suppose." He snickered again, his frail body shaking from the effort. "With my young, purty girlfriend." He was out-and out-laughing, completely amused by his own sad fantasy. "You make me smile, Nicholas."

"Glad to be of service." They made their way along the strip of rooms. The single-story building sat roadside, just outside of town. The peeling paint and the dirty windows turned away most law-abiding customers. It was a hangout for prostitutes and thugs. Not that there were a lot of them in the small mountain community, but there were enough.

The old man stopped at the next-to-last door and nodded toward the room on the end. "I know you ain't no regular cop, Nicholas, but you's a good'un." He handed Trent the key to the room. "I also knows this one is vermin." He started walking back toward the tiny office. "You won't mind dropping off the key on your way out, would ya?" He didn't look back or wait for a response.

Trent wondered idly what kind of "cop" the clerk thought he was. Vigilante? Fed? Didn't know. He looked at the door to that room and no longer cared.

Trent sniffed the air. The entire motel reeked of wet carpet and body odor. From outside, he couldn't pick out a particular scent if he had to. He leaned against the door, listening for movement in the room. Nothing.

He put the key in and turned it, trying to make as little noise as possible. The lock clicked loudly when the bolt withdrew, the door popping opened slightly. He grimaced at the racket. Trent stood still for an instant, straining to hear, feel or sense if he'd awakened Crey. He'd rather have blasted in, fangs showing. He waited a full minute. Still nothing.

He shoved the door all the way open. The bare bulb above the door partially illuminated the room. The bed was a mess, sheets hanging off on the floor. Towels were piled up next to the white plastic stand that held a decades-old television. Empty drink bottles and food cartons littered the tiny basin around the sink.

From the smell of the old food, it'd been sitting there for days. Chances were Crey had been gone just as long. Trent reached in and flipped the light switch. The place was an absolute mess. When he entered the room the hair on the back of his neck stood up. He smelled it clearly now. Blood magic.

He realized the bed was pushed from its normal spot against the center of a wall. It was shoved toward the door, making room for something on the far side. He stepped farther into the room, over the lump of sheets.

"Shit."

A circle was burned into the floor, inside it a five-pointed star. Large candles inside the circle marked the four directions of the earth. All had burned down to the base, wax spread out and hardened into solid puddles in the matted blue carpet.

Ash and stones were scattered throughout the circle. The rotting remains of a dead cat, its throat cut and blood spilled, lay over more ash, and moons only knew what else in the center. Trent saw a few bones, tiny and humanlike, peeking from beneath the cat's body. He nudged the stiff carcass slightly to the side and studied the small bones.

"Shit." He pulled out his cell. He searched through the contacts for a number he'd never before had to call and hit the send button.

"Location?" a stern female voice barked.

He gave her the address. "I've got a sacrifice."

There was no response. No conversation. Keys clattered in the background. "Can you hold the location for forty-five minutes?"

Trent looked around the deserted area. Keeping the old clerk away from the room would be no problem. More than likely he was already passed out. "Affirmative."

The line went dead.

He closed the door and glanced around the room. This sicko had definitely performed the spell on the human who'd attacked Nell. Trent's blood boiled at the thought.

He used his boot to push the cat remains farther off the pile. There were several of the tiny bones. He ground his teeth, fighting off his anger. His wolf was stretching, wanting to protect Nell. This guy was still out there.

He saw something shiny and red sticking out from under the bones and ash. He used his boot to nudge the pile harder, spreading out its contents. There was a chain of beads at the bottom. Red, yellow and black skull-shaped beads alternated around the length and a silver charm that looked like a dagger dangled from the center. He fished it out and tucked it in his pocket. He suspected Mi-ma might know what the chain of beads symbolized or where it came from. Then maybe he could track this guy.

He stepped back and saw markings carved in the vinyl floor of the bathroom area. Several crude skulls, a spiral, something that looked like a lizard and a couple other things he couldn't figure out at all. He memorized as much of the scene as possible to be able to share it with Mi-ma.

He should be sharing it with the Council, but he needed to get back to Nell as soon as possible. He couldn't protect *her* while he was sitting on his thumbs protecting a crime scene or in front of the Council sharing evidence.

The smell was getting to him. He stepped outside and locked the door behind him. He paced the length of the room along the walkway.

He should have never left her alone after the initial attack. And he certainly shouldn't have hurt her the way he had in the park. He ran his fingers through his thick hair. Damn his genetics. He closed his eyes and remembered how she felt in his arms, the smell of her skin as she rode him on that swing. He growled.

He knew if he gave in he'd go insane with wanting her. He'd always wanted her. It would be harder now. Now that she carried some of his blood, now that he had been inside her, felt her, loved her, Trent could no longer suppress his feelings. But he had to try. Had to push her away, make her leave town again, make her not want him, even *hate* him if that's what it took. He could live with her hating him, but he'd never be able to live with himself if he killed her.

And he would. Like his father had done to his mother, and his father before him. The burning jealousy, the Alpha temperament and the history was all the evidence he needed. His nature would not allow a normal life with a mate. The cycle would stop with him.

He ceased his pacing and banged his head against the metal door of the cheap motel room. "Get your head straight." There had been a serious attempt on Nell's life. He needed to concentrate on that. If he kept his mind on the job, he'd be okay. He'd discovered the *who*, now he needed the *why*. Crey had spun a spell that had possessed a human and tainted his blood. The Sorcerer was still out there. This guy was no simple lowlife, as Carson had said.

Trent glanced at his watch. Twenty more minutes.

* * * * *

With her reading glasses teetering on the end of her nose, Mi-ma inspected the box again. She carefully turned it this way and that, tapping here and there with the pad of her middle finger, listening to the sound of the wood as she went. They all watched without interrupting. All the granddaughters were tense, leaning forward at the long dining room table, waiting for a verdict. The only sound in the room was their grandmother's gentle tapping and the ticking of the kitchen clock.

She lowered the box as if she was going to speak...

And the doorbell rang. All four women jumped, Trina screamed and a sudden rush of adrenaline washed through Nell, making her heart pound and her toes tingle. She so loved that rush.

They all sat silent for a moment before Mi-ma burst out laughing.

"Who the heck is that?" Sonja asked.

Nell stood and headed toward the door, still enjoying the feel of the rush of being frightened. "Let's see, Miss Psychic, it's almost four a.m., we're holding something I'm sure the Council would love to get their hands on..." She looked over her shoulder and nodded at the box in warning. Sonja took her cue and slid it off the table, tucking it under her chair before Nell opened the door.

"And, we had a huge fight earlier. Care to guess?" she finished, swinging the door wide open. Trent stood there with his hands jammed in his pockets, as if it would make him look less imposing. "No one called you."

He started to walk in. Nell blocked his way. "I'm not here to talk to *you*. Not yet anyway." He didn't make eye contact.

Nell thought that rather cowardly and chose to point it out. "Are you going to lower your head every time you're around me from now on?" It was a sign of submission in the pack, and she knew it.

He met her accusing gaze. "No. I've had a very bad night, Nell, and I'm trying to keep it from getting worse by arguing with you now."

So...wild swing-set sex with her was a bad night for him? Ouch. Why did she let him hurt her so much?

He tilted his head. "Why are you covered in butterflies?"

She headed back to the table and her sisters, putting her back to him so she could hide the hurt she knew was showing in her eyes. "They, unlike others, are attracted to me, Prime. You can leave now."

"I need to talk to Mi-ma." He took several steps toward the table.

Mi-ma stood and reached for Nell. "Trenton Nicholas. You have some nerve. I don't know what's happened here — yet. But I can tell you did something stupid."

Nell let her grandmother embrace her. Coming back home had been a mistake. Coming back for *him* had been a bigger mistake. What had she been thinking?

Eight years. That's what she'd been thinking. Eight years should have been enough time for a young, headstrong Werewolf to mature. Instead, he had gotten more stubborn and more self-centered. She wished *she* weren't so stubborn. Then she wouldn't have set him up by tempting him in the park. Then she wouldn't know what his lips felt like as they peppered kisses on her neck. She now knew the thrill of his barely harnessed animal nature.

Over Mi-ma's shoulder, Nell saw Trina's face fall. Her youngest sister took a step back, stumbling over her chair. Nell turned to see Trent dangling a beaded chain between his fingers.

He looked past Nell to Trina. "You know what this is?"

Trina gathered herself. "Where did you get it?"

"It was in a motel room with the remnants of a very nasty ritual spell." He tucked it back in his pocket as if to shield them from its power. "There were human bones and a dead cat on the offering pyre. I was looking for the guy who attacked Nell. I found this in his room."

"Who is it?" Nell asked.

"A lowlife cretin named Crey. I have no idea why —"

Trina held up her hand to interrupt him. "Were there symbols painted on the walls in blood?"

Trent shook his head. "Carved in the floor." He looked at Mi-ma. "You have any paper? I can show her."

So, his night *had* sucked. Nell felt a little better that his comment hadn't referred only to his time with her. "Human bones?"

Sonja got a scrap of paper from the kitchen. Trent stepped toward Nell and nodded. He tried to soften his look, to no avail. Those features were all animal. She guessed he still hadn't changed, that his wolf was straining to get out. "Nell, this is serious. This is how the human you killed was possessed and his blood tainted. Do you have any idea why a blood-magic spell that powerful was aimed at you?"

She stepped back, away from him. "You asked me that a week ago and the answer is still no." Moths fluttered over her chest.

Trina spoke as Trent began drawing the symbols. "Santerian black magic. But that spell should've had to have been performed by a Palero. A very powerful Santerian priest."

"It was a scumbag Sorcerer." Trent shifted and Nell knew the moment he saw the box on the floor. His eyes got bigger.

"Where did that come from?" He glanced around the room. "What are you ladies up to?"

Sonja sat. Not so subtly, she pulled her chair a little farther under the table to hide the box better. "We're trying to comfort our sister."

Trent flinched but seemed to shake it off quickly.

Sonja smiled sweetly at him. "Some pain needs all the help it can get. You can leave us to our midnight mojitos and bitch session." She looked at Trina, who took the hint and scooted to the bar, started mixing drinks.

Trent looked at Sonja suspiciously. As he should, Nell thought. None of them could act their way out of a paper Witch's hat.

"Are you staying here tonight?" Trent crossed his arms and stood firm in the dining room.

Mi-ma sat back down. Nell didn't. "No."

"When were you planning on heading back home?" One of the moths flitted over and landed on his forehead. Sonja snickered. He scooted it off and it took flight briefly, only to land on the top of his head.

Nell raised an eyebrow. "Later."

"Nell, I *am* going to protect you. I lost Crey. I don't know if he's still on the mountain or not. You're going to be in protective custody until I figure this out."

"Go to hell." She figured it was Crey she'd shot in the basement. Judging from the amount of blood trailed out of there, he wasn't coming back soon.

"Nell."

She wanted to make him mad, to hurt him as he'd hurt her. It wasn't very mature but it was how she felt. "And just how do you expect to find this character if you're babysitting me? He's wounded. It's shouldn't be that hard to find him."

Trent scrunched up his face. "Nell..." It was more a growl than a spoken word. "How do you know that?"

Trina returned with a tray of lime-colored drinks.

"Thanks, Trina." Nell took a glass and sipped, not answering his question. The man really thought he could sweep in here and proclaim to be her protector and hero mere hours after rejecting her? The nerve.

Trent appeared to her grandmother. "Mi-ma, talk to her. This is dangerous magic. Somebody wants something." He nodded to the papers on the table. "I'm guessing you know more than I do at this point."

Mi-ma shook her head slightly. "You will do your job, Prime. She will fight you. In the end, all will be as it should."

Trent huffed and headed toward the door. "Demons." He stopped and turned back to them before exiting. "You're all hiding something. I know it."

Nobody answered until the door closed, then Sonja stuck out her tongue. "Pfffft." She looked at Nell. "I *am* really worried about this spell business."

Trina held out her hand. "It's all about the box, ladies." Sonja placed it on the table. "Nell, the moths are marking you as the messenger. You'll have to figure out the secrets of the box and its contents."

"But first we all need some sleep," Nell said. "Clearer minds will prevail." Nell scooped up the box and the papers. She was beat.

"You know he'll be following you. Probably camping outside your window," Trina said.

"Counting on it." Otherwise there was no way she'd go home. She was stubborn. Not stupid. "I'll make sure it's an enjoyable experience for him." Nell swung her backpack over her shoulder and drained the rest of her mojito. "Good night."

Trina hugged her. "Be careful."

"Be cool," Nell replied with an exaggerated point of the finger. It was the same lame reply she'd been giving her fire-starting sister for years.

* * * * *

Nell stepped into the kitchen, fresh out of the shower. Even though she'd washed his smell off her skin, she felt his presence like a blanket when she came down the stairs. The moths had left the confines of the basement and were now happily occupying the entire house. She had gotten used to them already. Trent's animal energy was another story. It was everywhere. He must have shifted. It made sense. He could easily hide in her garden or under the back deck and be very happy in his wolf form.

"Asshole." She said it loud enough that if he were close to the house, he'd hear it.

There was very little of the moon left, very little of the night. She was starving. After pouring a big bowl of Trix, she shook the empty milk carton then put it back in the fridge. Covering the cereal with lime yogurt seemed a viable alternative. She choked down the meager meal. Needing a drink, she poked around in the fridge and found a soda hiding behind some out-of-date tomato juice. Right behind that was a package of hamburger meat.

She snickered, grabbed the meat and another bowl. She plopped the raw meat into it and stepped out onto the back deck. She looked around but there was no sign of him. She tried to concentrate, to find his energy. She felt it, but couldn't narrow it to a location.

"Here, Trent," she called. "Come on boy. I got some yum-yums for you." She dropped the bowl onto the deck with a clank. "Come on, Trenton. Din-din." She headed back into the house, feeling a bit guilty. Maybe that had been a tad harsh, but he had acted like a dog. He'd made love to her and then rejected her. No "sorry", no "fuck you", no nothing. She thought she'd meant more to him than that. Even if he didn't love her, she deserved more than being tossed aside like yesterday's training paper. They'd grown up together in this small town.

She ran up the stairs and flopped onto her bed. The angry tears burst forth with her usual exuberant manner. It was an ugly cry and it felt great to let it out.

Moths gathered on her bed as her sobs receded. She felt as if she'd lost him, *really* lost him. It was similar to the pain of her father's death. She'd loved Trent so long, hoped and waited for years, knowing he would eventually feel the same way. Knowing he loved her too. Believing he was trying to think of his pack, or just being a young Alpha male who needed to live some before choosing his mate. She'd been patient and understanding, giving him time.

The knowledge that she'd been wrong, the realization that she could no longer think of her future as *their* future, left her empty. She closed her eyes to the rising sun.

She heard the clicking of nails on her stairs and the rustle of fur as he brushed past the doorjamb and entered her room. She knew the noise was intentional.

"I can't fight you anymore," she said without opening her eyes. She heard another rustling and felt the magic of his change push through the room. "I don't have anything left, Trent."

"I need to talk. I need to tell you." He was silent for a minute. She heard a large intake of breath, as if he were gearing up for something. "My father and my grandfather both killed their mates in fits of rage."

She head his footsteps cross her room. Nell held her breath.

"Probably my great-grandfather as well. It's a sickness. I have it too. I feel it constantly. Even when you were gone, I felt the constant jealousy. When Mi-ma told me you were living in that Vampire nest, I destroyed half an acre of trees. Took an axe to them. Hacked for hours."

"I—"

"Nell, let me speak, please." His voice was soft.

She stayed still and kept her eyes closed.

"I've always loved you. And I have always fought to keep you far enough out of my life to keep you safe. I don't want to hurt you. I didn't want to know what it was like to feel your body. Because I was afraid once we were intimate, I wouldn't be able to resist. And then I'd be destined to repeat the sins of my fathers. I can't, Nell. I can't be what you need, what you deserve."

Nell had heard stories about his mother's death in high school, but considered them rumors based in teenage angst. She'd never even asked Mi-ma or her father about them.

So all this was to keep from hurting her? All these years?

"I'm trying to protect you, not only from Crey, but from myself."

More tears started rolling down her face. She had been self-centered. In all this time, she had never considered he might have serious reasons for shutting her out. She had thought she knew and understood her wolf.

She was wrong. This changed everything.

She thought back to the last time he'd rejected her, back when they were kids really, and it had felt as if the world were ending. He'd been a jerk then too, intentionally pushing her away. Trying to get her to go on with her life even though he'd loved her. A romantic gesture, sure, but...

"Do you think I can just quit?" She wasn't sure if he was still in the room or not. He was still close. Trent wouldn't leave her vulnerable to Crey, she knew that, but was he still in the room?

She sat up to check. He stood at the end of the bed. He looked even more tired than she felt.

"You have to, Nell." His eyes were pleading. "I don't have the willpower anymore. I proved that on the playground. I can't stand not touching you. At the same time, I can't stand the thought of hurting you. I need you to do this for us, Nell."

She'd never seen him show weakness to anyone. It broke her heart. "Come lie down."

He closed his eyes and let his shoulders drop. "That's not exactly helpful."

"Just this once. I've been up for something like thirty-six hours. I'm sure you have as well. Let's just lie here and take a nap. Tomorrow, later on, whatever, we'll figure out the rest." She held her arms open. "Just this once, let me hold you."

Trent stood still for a moment. But she saw when his will broke. He stepped forward, crawled onto the bed and scooted toward her. Moths scattered. Nell wrapped her arms around him and held him tight against her chest as they lay back.

There was no way she was giving up on him. Not now.

* * * * *

Her rhythmic breathing lulled him to sleep. Her roaming hands woke him. Trent had no idea what time it was, only that it seemed late in the day. He remained perfectly still, his muscles tight with anticipation, eyes closed. He should get up and go. Hell, he should run. But her hand was sliding south and his temperature was heading north. She was dreaming, her head on his chest. Her body was moving, reacting to an alternate reality in her mind, rocking gently against his side. He held his breath as her fingers made their way down his stomach.

The heat of Nell's body and the feel of the soft sheets under his back were heaven. This was how it should be. How it *would* be if he didn't have the monkey on his back. At that thought, he *did* try to sit up.

Nell groaned as she clung to his abdomen. "No," she complained. "Not yet. I was dreaming."

He knew exactly what she was dreaming and his body might as well have been in the dream realm with her. She ran her fingers through the hair that was a mere inch from his growing erection.

He sat up, easing her back onto a pillow as he did. She curled up on her side, hugging the pillow. "Nell." He shook his head as she opened her fawn-colored eyes. Her golden curls were a wild mess spread on the white sheets.

She batted her eyelashes to clear the sleep and Trent about lost it. He loved this woman. How could he resist her?

"I can't." He spoke the words but his hand drifted to the curve of her breast. He could make out her nipple under the thin t-shirt she wore. He ran his fingers down her side, shooing a couple moths as he went. "I can't."

She rolled onto her back, stretching out her legs, stretching her arms over her head, giving him a full view of her body. She reached out her hand. Trent had still been nude from his change when he'd collapsed onto the bed. In hindsight, sleeping with her in his naked state wasn't the smartest move for a man who needed to keep his distance from this particular temptation. Nell was not a shy wallflower. No. She reached right for his aching cock and wrapped her small fingers around it.

A satisfied smile crossed her lips as she stroked him. Trent thought his head was going to explode. His mind was reeling with years' worth of fantasies of Nell Ambercroft in his bed. The swing set had been nice, but it had also been unexpected and the sex driven by his wolf. Now she was supple and sweetly willing. He had an opportunity he never thought he'd get. To relax and explore her.

She released his swollen cock and sat up long enough to strip off her shirt before falling back. Her breasts bounced with the movement. They were full but not huge. He ran his hand over her stomach. Her tummy had a lovely swell at the bottom of her abdomen. He loved the curves. All her curves.

He caressed her skin, making his way back up her side and taking the weight of one of her breasts in his hand. Her fingers found their way back to him, cupped his balls and lightly squeezed. Trent closed his eyes and let his head fall back. For a moment he knew he should object, stop this madness. He knew what was going to happen. He would never be able to forget her like this. He'd be driven mad trying to stay away, continually yo-yoing in and out of her life. In the process, he'd drive *her* mad by his weakness and lack of resolve.

As much as he wanted to be strong enough to walk away, at this moment, with her naked and stroking him, he wasn't able.

He leaned down and kissed her with all the emotion and expression he could deliver. He probed her hot mouth with his tongue, exploring, taking. She cupped his head, eagerly returning the kiss. He felt her desire and her need. He shifted and pressed his body to hers, wanting to feel as much of his skin touching hers as possible. Using his knee, Trent pushed her legs apart and then wriggled between them. He covered her, could feel her from his lips to his ankles. Her smell, a combination of sage and morning dew, was imprinted in his brain.

He was mated.

He pulled away from her lips and kissed the sides of her face, one cheek at a time. From her cheeks, he brushed his lips over one earlobe, sucking it gently into his mouth, blowing light breaths in her ear. She shivered under him.

Her neck tasted earthy and fresh, her skin clean, no perfumes, no unnatural scents to infiltrate his sensitive sense of smell. It made him want her even more; his cock was about to burst and he'd not even made it to her breasts yet.

"God. Trent." She pushed on his shoulders to hurry him along.

"Hush. Just feel, baby." Moths were flitting around overhead, uncertain where to land with his body covering hers. A couple landed on his back and somehow that felt right as well. "Just feel."

She arched under him, urging with her body. He licked over a collarbone, inching down, touching and teasing her neck as he moved. When he finally reached her breasts, he raised up to look at them. Her nipples were taut from desire, the color of brown sugar. He reached out a pointed tongue and flicked over one hard peak.

He heard her sharp intake of breath and drew that nipple into his mouth. She was writhing. Her hips moving under him were an invitation that was hard to ignore. But he wanted to take his time, to love her body, to give to her this one slow, relaxed experience.

He moved to the other breast, peppered light kisses across the top, brushing her nipple with his lips then rubbing his face over the soft, golden skin. He wanted to drive her to new heights, to push her enough to see a bit of her Demon.

He looked to the bedside table. "Nelly, I can't believe there are no toys sitting out."

She glanced to the table and back to him. She looked unsure but her eyes gave away her interest.

"Are they all in the chest?"

She shook her head. "Drawer."

Trent scooted back up to reach inside the nightstand drawer, his chest even with her face. As he stretched toward the drawer, she licked his nipple. Hesitating, he looked at her just before she bit down. He growled low and closed his eyes. Her lips felt good on his skin. Continuing his quest, he opened the drawer to find two vibrators. He wasn't exactly inexperienced, but he'd not really used toys in his sexual exploits. He took out a small rubber vibrator. It was clear blue and not much larger than his thumb. It would do the trick.

Resuming his position, he kissed and nibbled each breast again, making sure she was good and bothered. Nell's body temperature rose. Her breathing increased in pace. And Trent was getting as excited as she was. He moved lower, kissing, licking and blowing cool air across her tummy. Gooseflesh rose in the wake of his attentions. She reached out, grabbing the sheets and arching toward him, urging him lower still.

"I'm getting there. Don't you worry." He moved again, down between her legs. She parted them eagerly, looking at him down the length of her body. Her eyes had darkened. Her face was flushed.

"Can I see the Demon, Nell? Can you let that Dragon come partially through? Or do you have to fully change?"

"I can control it most of the time."

He smiled and cocked an eyebrow. "Most?"

She shrugged. "Halfling." She raised her hips and rolled them in a sexy, teasing manner. "I could cross the line, fully shift at an unwanted time. But even then it's not much of a shift compared to yours."

The thought of Nell shifted and primal made him even more desirous.

She shook her head. "It's not a sexy state for me though."

"No?" He pressed a light kiss over her swollen mound.

"Yes. No." She lifted her hips slightly in invitation to continue, to delve further. "Partial is good. I'm very aware. Once I go into full Demon mode, I'm all instinct. It's really hard to focus."

He kissed her again, letting his tongue linger and part her labia before raising his head. "Not good for you when it's all instinct?"

She whimpered. "Not really. I'm kind of fight-or-flightish. Not sensory like your wolf."

His wolf would love this. But shifting and sex was not cool. At least not in *his* mind. There were those who did, but he wanted to feel all this in his human form. The wolf had better night vision and a better sense of smell, but his human skin, his human fingers, were all about touch and feel. Nell Ambercroft had much to touch and feel.

He twisted the little vibrator to start it up. She moaned at the sound of it humming. He touched it to her clit and she spread her legs wider, her scent enveloping him. He kissed her thigh and watched as her sex moistened. She eased her hand down and attempted to touch herself.

"Oh no you don't. Grab the headboard. Let me play, Nell."

"Trent. I want to come already. Please."

He shook his head, letting his lips brush her mound again. "Nope. I want *this*." She closed her eyes and let her head fall back. She gripped the rustic iron bars on the headboard.

"Spread for me." Nell followed his orders. Positioning her legs as wide as she could, opening her treasures for him. He was about to burst. He wanted to lift up and plunge in. He wanted to fuck her right then. But he refrained.

He touched her with the vibrator again, circling her clit and spreading her wetness. He pressed the vibrator just inside her and then teased her clit with his mouth. She moaned and bucked. He held the toy there, humming away.

"Trent!"

"Can you do it, baby? Can I see your Dragon?" He'd seen hints of it before, the Dragon her father had passed on to her. Her nature. The animal inside that made her *more*. It was golden and powerful, even if she didn't have the ability to completely control it.

"If I go too far…"

He moved the vibrator back to her clit, pressing, and she tried to pull away from the intensity. He stayed with her.

Nell let go of the headboard and grasped the sheets. She let her back arch high and let the Dragon show. He saw it first in the lush skin of her inner thighs. Her skin seemed to stretch the smallest bit. Just below the surface, her Demon's Dragon slithered. It had golden, shimmering scales that pulsed with her Demon magic.

Trent was lost in the exotic, rich feel of that magic. He dropped the vibrator and crawled up her body. Kissing his way up the length of her stomach and chest. Admiring her skin. Her smell had changed from sage and dew to a floral scent mixed with a hint of hot metal.

He captured her mouth with his, kissing her hard. With his hips, he pushed his way inside her. The move wasn't exactly gentle, but he was on the edge and she was partially shifted. Gentle no longer appealed to him. She opened her eyes and gripped his back, digging nails into his skin. He growled.

She squeezed him as he remained ensconced inside her. He wanted to take just a moment to memorize the feel of her wrapped around his shaft. He was shaking with the effort of not moving.

"Go." It was little more than a whisper but he followed the command as if she had shrieked it. He pulled out and plunged in again and again. He let himself get lost in the sensations, in the primal bonding that lovemaking could bring.

She made a growling sound of her own and Trent worried that he would push her over the edge to a full shift. He wanted this to be just as good for her. He slowed. "Nell. Baby. Look at me."

She worked to open her eyes, to focus on him. Bright green irises with a rim of silver and reptilian slits for pupils had replaced her usual light brown eyes. He kissed her. She kissed back as she shifted once more to her human form. She gripped the muscles of his back, pulled away from the kiss. Her body writhed with his every move. Her moans had turned to wanting whimpers. He felt her pussy tighten around his cock.

"Come for me." He quickened the pace just a tad.

Shit. She was exquisite in this state. Her flushed face was glowing. Her curves sexy and moving with the rhythm of his body. He was going to come first if he wasn't careful. He leaned in and took a ripe nipple in his lips and bit down gently before sucking it into his mouth.

Nell let out a scream and shoved him as deep as he could go. He felt her explode. He didn't hold back any longer. He followed her orgasm with his own.

He held her tight. Feeling her body shudder, feeling her heart beat against his chest. Feeling his love for her. How was he going to give her up?

Chapter Seven

ℬ

She felt his withdrawal long before she felt his body start moving. Nell held her comments as he pulled away. Her first instinct was to shout, yell at him. Insist that she knew better, that she knew he would never hurt her. At least, he'd never hurt her in a physical way. The two of them had been hurting each other for years. He didn't speak as he slipped into the hall bathroom. She listened as the shower started. Had his father and grandfather really been responsible for their mates' deaths? Only one person on this side of the mountain would know that bit of information for sure.

Moths resettled after all the commotion of their lovemaking. She inspected one as she lay in the bed. "I have to figure out why you ladies have taken up residence with me. I'm not the best of ecosystems. You must be getting hungry." She got up and pulled her t-shirt back on and grabbed some shorts. She needed to solve two separate mysteries. Both required the wolf not be hanging around. That was going to be difficult since he was on a mission to protect her from this Crey character.

She stuck her head into the bathroom. She could see his silhouette through the shower curtain. The man was a hottie. His ass was high, tight and round. She wanted to go over and squeeze it. "Can I use your cell?"

"Sure. In my jeans on the back deck."

Downstairs, she fumbled through his jeans for the phone then brought his clothes inside and dumped them on the table. How to get rid of a determined Werewolf? She dialed her grandmother.

Mi-ma answered on the first ring. "Are you two finished already?"

Nell scrunched her face even though her grandmother couldn't see it. "Finished? With what?" She didn't have time to make cute small talk. "I need to talk to you about Trent." She looked up toward the stairs. "And we need to open this box."

Nell heard Sonja's voice in the background but couldn't make out her words. Mi-ma spoke to Sonja. "That's what *I* said. They're already done." Was the whole family sitting there waiting to hear about her sex life? "We'll be there in two shakes of a wolf's tail."

"Mi-ma. I need to ask you—" The line went dead. So much for answers while Trent was in the shower. The water shut off. A few minutes later he headed down the stairs.

Nell made her way into the shower and turned the water on as hot as she could stand. She wanted his smell off her. She wanted to think straight. Yes, she wanted him and loved him and needed to understand his history better, but right now her life was at stake and that meant box and murder attempts before hearts and love lives. She'd waited this long for Trent. A few more days weren't going to kill her. She hoped.

Plotting, she quickly dressed in a tight camisole and loose jeans. She brushed through her hair before twisting it into a knot to hold it out of her face. Having all her hair pulled up gave her a dramatic look. She put on a tiny bit of eye shadow and mascara to complete the image. It wasn't exactly makeup for going out on the town, but it would work.

He was on the couch thumbing through an old cooking magazine when she got to the bottom of the stairs. His stomach growled. "I'm hungry too." She went into the kitchen and made a deliberate show of checking the fridge and the pantry. "Nothing here." She leaned over the bar, letting her crossed arms push her breasts up, giving her more cleavage. "Why don't you run to Tommy's and get us a pizza? Pepperoni and black olive."

He flipped the page. "I'm not leaving, Nell." He didn't even look up to see the cleavage.

"We have to eat. I'm *starving*."

He closed the magazine and stood. "Then we go together."

"I have to wait for —"

Mi-ma marched through the front door at that moment with a large tea pitcher in her hand. Sonja and Trina followed behind her like little ducks. Sonja had a big white bag and Trina had two large pizza boxes from Tommy's.

Of all the times for Sonja's psychic abilities to be dead-on. She scratched the base of her hairline at the back of her head. Her grandma and sisters started setting out the food, oblivious to Nell's attempt to rid herself of one wolf.

They ate, her sisters chattering on about the local gossip and news as if nothing were amiss. Trent was back on the couch, listening, rolling his eyes and huffing. Apparently gossip of the local dating scene wasn't his idea of scintillating conversation.

Nell grabbed him another slice from the box and absentmindedly started pulling off the olives. She caught his eyes on her. She *did* know her wolf.

It'd been ten years since they'd had pizza together and she remembered he didn't like black olives. She knew he was allergic to shellfish and that he had a scar on his knuckles from beating up the class bully after he pushed Nell in the hall. She saw those same memories pass through his eyes. She also saw the pain. Did Trent really believe he'd hurt her, possibly even kill her?

Trina poured Nell some more tea. "You remember when I set my back deck on fire the last time?"

Nell nodded. The poor girl had a fire or two a month. She'd sneeze and the curtains would light up like sparklers.

Trina continued. "That Linda Newcomb, she came rushing over as soon as the fire truck got there."

Sonja huffed out a laugh. Nell just listened, silently encouraging Trina to keep talking, knowing full well gossip drove Trent out of his mind.

"She practically stripped for Howard Henderson. He had burned his hand but it was no worse than a sunburn, really. Well, Linda basically ripped off her shirt to wrap it up. As if no one knows they're as fake as that bowl of fruit on Mi-ma's kitchen table."

Nell glanced over to see Trent drop the magazine and head to the front door.

Well…outside was better than nothing.

* * * * *

The basement had been nothing more than storage for years, but her father must have spent some time down here. Behind one of the racks stacked with boxes and tomes, she found an old glass lamp. She pulled the table nearer to an outlet and plugged in the lamp, the glow in the room now much more pleasant and golden. She let out a small huff of relief and triumph.

The moths were still attracted to the destroyed box and to Nell's skin. Mi-ma came down with a fresh drink. Trina followed. "Pizza's put away." Both women sat at the table.

Sonja came down shortly thereafter. "So what is it with the moths?"

Trina urged one of the moths onto her hand. "They're huge, aren't they?"

"They're also starting to get on my nerves." Nell pulled her laptop out of her backpack and set it next to the lamp. She plugged in a wireless access card and waited for a signal. "I need a little more info about these ladies."

"You can get internet with that thing here?" Mi-ma asked.

"Yep. I can connect to any mobile phone signal in the area. It can be a little slow way out here, but it works." She typed in a search for the moths. "Came in handy when I was traveling so much."

"I bet." Sonja sat next to her while the others thumbed through more documents that had spilled from the cardboard container.

Nell picked up the wooden box to study it further. She closed her eyes and ran her hand over the texture of the wood. She was tempted to try using her telekinesis to blast it open, and then thought better of it. That would make a mess of the box and probably its contents as well.

One of the moths made its way to the end of Nell's hand as she felt her way along the ridges of a grain of reddish wood…

Of course!

She concentrated. A shape began to feel alive under her fingers and in her mind. She opened her eyes and smiled. "Here ya go, little sister." She urged the moth onto the box.

"What are you thinking?" Trina asked.

"Hang on and we'll see." Nell scooted the moth a bit forward with her finger, turning her to the right. When the Black Witch was in just the right spot, she stopped and spread her wings as far as they could, shaking them as if to dry them.

"I'll be," Mi-ma whispered as the moth began to take on a golden glow. "The moths are part of the box."

The light emitted was enough to brighten the room. The women all had to squint to watch as the moth turned golden, the intricate outlines and details of her wings hardening into gilded sculpture — and then melding into the box.

Nell traced the outline of the golden moth with her fingertips. She turned the box over a couple times, looking to see if that had triggered anything. "Huh. Not opening it. Must need more than one." She tried to find another spot that looked like an outline of a moth in the grains of the mixed woods.

"Close your eyes and feel for it again, Nelly," Sonja said. "See it with your other senses."

Nell did as Sonja suggested, using her fingers to feel the lines and swirls. After a moment, she found another one. She marked the spot with one hand and retrieved a moth with the other and coaxed her into place. Immediately, the moth began to transform into a golden incarnation.

"This could take a while if you have to cover the entire thing," Trina said. "I'll get some more tea."

Nell glanced up the stairs, wondering just how long Trent was going to stay outside. She closed her eyes and started the search for the next place to put a moth on the box. The room was quiet. "Mi-ma? Did Trent's dad and grandpa really kill their mates?"

"Yes. Yes, they did," Mi-ma said, her voice distant, melancholy.

"Concentrate on the box, Nell," Trina said. "Trent will be back soon. I'm sure he's not that far away as it is."

Nell felt the faint outline of a wing. She urged another moth into place. As the insect shimmered into gold, Nell looked at Mi-ma.

"I have to understand. He's shutting me out." She closed her eyes and started to feel for the next spot. Her ability to find the designs in the wood seemed to come faster each time. The moths were swarming around her again, each clamoring to be the next piece of the puzzle. She felt their collective magic.

"I don't know the particulars of his grandmother's death. For years I heard rumors of Cedric, his grandfather, being a mean drunk. They say he lost his mind with rage one night over something silly at a ceremony for the pack. That he got jealous and tore her limb from limb. But that's a forty-year-old rumor. We weren't close enough back then to know much about inter-pack problems."

Nell managed to find another spot and keep up with Mi-ma's story. "And his father? I think he was already gone when I first remember Trent in school."

"He was. Trent was no more than seven or eight when it all happened." She shook her head and looked to the ceiling. "Was a sad day, it was. Arly, his dad, was the Alpha. Even with the rumors of Cedric's problems. He married a woman named Ednas, from another pack. It was a smart move because she was the daughter of that pack's Alpha. The marriage brought strength and allies to both packs. Ednas was widowed and had a young son named Cole."

"I don't remember Trent having a step-brother," Trina said as she came down the stairs with a tray of tea.

"Well. Cole stayed over on Barton's Ridge, up near West Virginia. That's where his kin lived, including his Alpha grandfather." She took a long sip of her drink. Nell felt around for the next moth slot while watching Mi-ma's animated face. "You see, the grandfather didn't want that boy around Ednas. She was crazy as a loon and the old Alpha knew it. So he married her off to Arly and made her *his* problem."

Always the dramatic storyteller, Mi-ma surveyed their faces to make sure all three girls were enthralled before continuing. "Only thing was, that crazy bitch was also damn evil." She looked pointedly at Nell. "She gave Arly a son of his own, but she wanted her first son, Cole, to have both packs when he matured. She wanted Trent out of the picture because he was in line for Alpha of his father's pack. So the lunatic cooked up a plan. She took the whole family on an outing to a cabin up near Pilot Mountain. She waited until they were all asleep—and then she set the cabin on fire."

Trina gasped and covered her mouth. "With the boys inside?"

"The boys and Arly. Apparently, while he slept, she'd moved Cole close to the front door where she could get to him easily. She'd only intended on Trent and Arly burning up."

Trina looked as though she where on the verge of tears. Nell's sister spent most her life protecting others from her abilities. The thought of using fire as a weapon, on purpose, shocked her. "What happened, Mi-ma?"

Nell had stopped her progress with the box, wondering the same thing.

"Well, from what I understand, Trent woke up while she was splashing the gas around. He questioned her, as any child would if he found his mother pouring gasoline all over the divan. Arly came in just as she tried to splash the stuff directly on Trent. Arly, being at his wits end with his loco wife, dragged her out to the woods to get her away from the kids. She attacked him. They both shifted. He killed her dead."

"Oh my," Nell breathed, slowly turning the box over to find another location. Another moth glowed golden and then melded with the wood. "But what happened to the brother?"

Mi-ma gave a slow shake of her head. "With all that gasoline everywhere, something sparked the fire. The adults were out in the woods fighting." She let out a sympathetic sigh. "Her plan backfired, 'cause Cole was the one who didn't find his way out. Bless his heart." She looked at Nell. "But Trent did."

They were all quiet for a moment. Nell saw that Trina was still fighting back tears. Fire deaths always affected her badly.

Nell wondered what Trent actually remembered from that night. The rumors that had circulated in high school sounded more like Trent's version, that his father was abusive and a murderer.

"Where is Arly now?" Sonja asked.

Mi-ma shrugged her shoulders. "He left shortly after it happened. No one knows for sure. I suspect Trent could find him if he really wanted."

Trina got up. She paced the length of the basement, stopping at the broken, dingy window. "Wow. So sad."

"Closing in here," Nell said as another moth transformed into gold. The back was covered in intricate reliefs of the moths. The front was mostly covered; there were only about three spots left.

How could she broach what she'd learned with Trent? *You know, your dad did kill your mother, but she was a loco bitch who deserved it for trying to kill you.* Sounded a bit, well…just as bad as saying his dad was an abuser. She wasn't sure it would help her case. Nope. Trent would have to figure out on his own who he was, and whether he needed her enough to fight through his fears. She couldn't force it on him and she couldn't change his view of his world. Trent would have to come to *her*.

She wondered just how much longer she was willing to wait.

She'd told Trent in anger that she was done with him and his brooding Alpha self. And perhaps she should be. But she could feel him, even now.

* * * * *

Trent watched from his perch on the top step. The pack of women rambled on about him and his history. He'd heard lots of versions of what had happened with his family. Most came from folks who had no reason to have a version of his life events at all—kids at school, neighbors, drunks and scumbags in the local taverns. He guessed they were pretty bored if they still wanted to talk about his history.

Mi-ma's account of that night was very different from the versions his classmates and the other Weres had used over the years. It was an interesting take on things. The old Demon was like an all-knowing mountain Buddha. There was a good chance her story was closer to the truth than most others.

Another moth turned into its golden doppelganger and melted into the box. He should interrupt them now. But he wanted to see what happened when the box was completely covered in gold.

No matter how much he'd tried to remember the events of the night his mother had died, Trent had no recollection, so he'd never know for sure. And it didn't matter. His mom was dead. His father killed her. If she was crazy enough to try to kill her own child, then he had bad genes from both sides of the family. He hated the pity on Trina's face.

"Last one," Nell proclaimed. They all gathered around the table. He could see the box over Nell's shoulder. The single remaining spot was in the center. They all seemed to be holding their breath. He noted that he was too.

She placed her hand on the spot. Several of the moths circled, bumping into one another, making shadows dance across the women and the table. The air that had been moving though the room from the open window to the open door at the top of the stairs stilled.

Finally, she raised her hand into the small swarm of remaining moths. One landed on her forearm. It was a big one. Bright blue and silver laced its wingspan. It looked more like a glimmering fairy than an insect.

She placed her hand back on the edge of the box. Like a flame, the box was irresistible to the moth. It crawled its way down her arm. She turned her hand slightly as it stepped onto the box to keep it on course. It fluttered its wings and turned itself to the right. Nell coaxed it back to the correct position. It turned itself a little to the left, not moving forward or back, just spinning in the open spot.

They all watched as it stood there, a little cockeyed to the moth-shaped spot that remained.

The glowing didn't start right away, as it had with the others. Sonja glanced around at all the others and then back to the moth. None of the rest of them had taken their eyes off the box or the bug.

Nell sat back. "Now what?"

Trina rushed to the table. Trent stood and glanced around for what may have spooked her. The others tensed.

"Get back,'" she ordered. They followed her instructions without question, moving a step or two away from the table and the box. Even Trent stiffened, ready to intervene if needed. Mi-ma glanced at him but didn't give him away.

"It's going to burn," Trina said.

No sooner were the words out of her mouth than a small fire ignited with a flash under the moth. She didn't move or resist the flame, just went up like a pint-sized phoenix. Bright orange flames with glowing blue tips engulfed the Black Witch. The brightened room reminded Trent of a dingy, neon-lit tavern. The rest of the moths in the room lit up like giant fireflies dancing on a hot June evening.

"Whoa," Sonja said as she stepped back to the table to get a closer look at the burning moth. Trina also moved closer to the flame.

A beam shot out of the top of the moth like a searchlight. It blasted the room with an explosive percussion, pushing the women back away from the table and temporarily blinding Trent.

When his eyes adjusted, the light in the room had returned to normal, the flame was gone and the moth was a golden statue standing on top of the box. It hadn't melded into the wood. And this golden moth was *very* different.

"Crap! Is that a diamond?" Nell gasped.

"Goodness," Mi-ma said. "I believe so."

Chapter Eight

ဢ

The teardrop-shaped diamond was the biggest Trent had ever seen. Not that he was an expert by any means but the stone that now made up the body of the moth had to be the size of his thumb.

Nell started to reach for the box. Sonja held out both her hands in warning. "Before you touch anything, let me take a picture." She reached into her back pocket to retrieve her cell phone.

"Good idea," Nell said as Sonja snapped a few photos.

Trent wasn't sure *any* of this was a good idea. And it was time he let the gathering of Halflings know it. "Do you have the slightest inkling what you're about to do?" he asked as he stomped down the stairs.

Nell answered without looking back. Maybe she'd known he was sitting there all along. Maybe she'd known when Mi-ma was telling the tale of his parents' fall from grace. He wasn't sure how he felt about that, though really, it didn't matter what Nell knew. Her opinion on the subject had no relevance. Nothing had changed. He was still who he was no matter the circumstances of his mother's death.

"Yes. I do." She pulled the box closer.

Mi-ma stood and pressed her hands to the back of her hips. She leaned back in an exaggerated stretch. "What's your concern? It's a puzzle box. It means to be solved and opened."

"A cobra means to bite too," Trent said as he leaned over the table and examined the box more carefully. "That doesn't mean I want to be on the receiving end of the biting."

Mi-ma barked out a loud laugh, half-hacking, half-cackling. "You crack me up, young man."

"Don't you suppose we should find out what this is before we open it?" Trent directed his attention fully to Nell, not giving Mi-ma or either of the sisters a chance to interject.

"Look. I was attacked over this thing. I'm going to figure out why." She lifted the box, turning it. The crazy moths were now in gold relief on the outside and Trent could make out the tiniest of seams along the side. The diamond-bodied moth stood above the last of the bug-shaped puzzle spaces.

"Gee, you think it might be the giant diamond?" He was trying to sound imposing. It didn't work.

"Trent," Nell sighed but looked at her sister. Sonja nodded her head. Nell set the box on the table and pushed the last moth down into place on the wood. She squealed and yanked her hand away, shaking and blowing on her palm.

"You okay?" Mi-ma asked.

"Burned me." Nell continued to blow on her hand. "I'm fine."

The box released a gush of air that sounded like a great exhale, as though it were relieved to be opened. Then, as if on a set of springs, the box opened like a golden clam.

The smell of blood magic filled the basement, making Trent's shoulders tighten. The women all leaned over the box. He couldn't see a thing.

"Is that bone?" Trina asked.

"I think so," Mi-ma said. "Lots of African Voodoo talismans are carved out of bone or ivory."

Trent worked his way between Nell and Sonja. A necklace rested inside the box, suspended just above the bottom as if in a display case. The chain was decorated with little skulls, teeth and feathers. In the center, a brilliant, forest-green stone with deep red flecks hung from a braided black loop.

Mi-ma took Nell's hand. "Let me see your hand, girl."

"It's fine. Just a small burn." Nell let her grandmother open her hand.

"Burn?" Trina said. "Jeez-Louise, Nelly. You've been branded."

"It's fine." Nell studied the burn for a moment. It was the perfect shape of the moth. She grabbed her laptop and looked to Sonja. "Email me that picture of the moth and take another photo of the beads."

She was typing away on her computer before Trent had a chance to interject. "Nell. We need to discuss this. I have a responsibility to the Council. I need to be in control of this."

Nell's computer rang like a phone. Video call. Crap. The fact that this family was part of his life and he had feelings for Nell had impaired his official judgment.

"Wow! Nelly. You look great, love," a male voice with an English accent sang from the other end of the cyber connection. Trent's skin crawled.

"You too, Robin. How's Jeania?"

"Tops. She's..." There was a slight hesitation and a few keyboard clicks in the background. "Nelly, is this thing in your possession?" Nell nodded at the laptop. "What have you gotten yourself into this time, love?"

"I don't like the sound of that," Trina said.

Trent bent forward to be seen by the little camera. "What is it?" The question came out in a growling voice.

The image of Robin on the screen looked at Trent. "Who is that hunk of a Were and what are you up to, my golden Dragon?"

Trent wanted to rip apart the image on the screen. He didn't have a playful nickname for Nell. Hell, he didn't have *any* nickname for her. How did this guy know her Demon form was a Dragon?

A beautiful redhead poked her head over the man's shoulder. "Hello, Nelly," she said in a heavy French accent. She kissed Robin on the cheek.

"Jeania!" Nell proclaimed with glee. "*Amour du mien.*" She blew the woman a kiss.

"*Manquez-vous*, Nelly," the woman said. Trent didn't understand the words, but the woman looked very sad. "Is that your Werewolf?"

Nell looked over her shoulder at him. Her eyes also slipped into sadness. "I guess not," she said back to the screen.

Trent felt his stomach sink. So the entire world knew of their relationship—or *lack* of a relationship. He didn't have time to deal with his emotions at the moment. He steeled his spine. "The necklace? You know something about it?"

"Ah. Yes. It's the Chiwa talisman. The Beads of Death. A very powerful Voodoo talisman, or gris-gris. Rumor has it that one of the most powerful Palero priests in the world used the Chiwa to change the history of Cuba. A powerful human warlord owned the thing but had no magic to use its power. He traded that talisman to the Palero priest, who performed a spell that started a revolution. Rumor, of course."

Robin went on. "The skulls are supposedly carved from the bones of babes, sacrificed in nasty, inhuman ways. The ritual bloodletting gives the beads their power. It is bad mojo, Nelly." He pointed at her through the screen and waved his finger back and forth. "Do not handle it any more than you have to. That huge piece of jasper hanging from it boosts energy and magical power, even yours. However, it won't boost your ability to *control* that power."

Christ, Trent thought. That's all he needed was this bunch to get a mega-boost of their dubious Demon gifts. The three of them could destroy this side of the mountain if that happened.

Trina stepped back to the window, away from the Beads of Death. The fire starter must have been thinking the same thing, because she looked like she wanted to get out of the room.

Nell grabbed the golden moth box and held it in front of the camera where Robin could see it. "What about this? The two don't seem to go together. A golden puzzle box and an African Voodoo necklace?" Trent wondered the same thing.

"Hmm. Turn it over." Robin rubbed his finger over his upper lip. "I'm not positive. It looks to be a copy of Egyptian construction, but the moths are reminiscent of South African lore. I don't think it's an antiquity, Nelly. Someone devised that recently. Very likely for the sole purpose of housing that necklace, to hide it."

"Really?" Nell asked, looking it over again. "Thanks for the help. You guys are the greatest." She kissed the air twice. "And I miss you too, Jeania."

Trent heard Nell sigh. It wasn't the male Nell was attached to—it was the female.

The redhead stuck her face back in front of the camera. Her green eyes were full of tender emotion. "Come back to Paris, Nelly. I am only half without you. If *his* heart is not yours, you know mine is."

"Jeania," Nell said with a fake French accent, "you sexy bitch. Quit teasing me. You'd never give up the rest of the nest and settle down with one simple Demon."

"Ha!" The Vampire laughed. "Nothing simple about you."

Trent shook his head. Had they had a relationship? Nell's tone was joking, but he heard a hint of truth in the French woman's voice and he definitely saw real affection in those green eyes. He knew that look, understood its cause. She wanted Nell.

He pushed his fingers through his hair and scratched the back of his head. Nell sat in front of him, a few inches away. And he wanted her badly. He could reach out, put his hand on her shoulder and feel her skin. Simply to have his hand there would be a physical connection and maybe it would be enough for him at this moment.

He doubted it, and it wouldn't be fair to her.

The two women said their goodbyes as if Robin weren't there. He interjected his goodbyes just before ending the call. Trent pulled his brain away from Nell and her friends. He needed to be in investigative mode.

He ran the facts through his mind. He had a dead human, an Egyptian puzzle box with what looked to be a real diamond as the key, a Voodoo talisman reeking of serious blood magic and Crey, the creep of a Sorcerer who, by reputation, hadn't the brains to manage either. Was he after money or power? Trent supposed it really didn't matter. Crey was trying to hurt Nell either way. And Trey would love to get his hands on the guy.

Until then, the council needed to be brought in. This was too big now for him to keep under wraps. The dangerous necklace needed to be in safe hands. "I need to take this to the Council. They're meeting this weekend."

Nell spun around with her brows pinched and her eyes on fire. She'd gone from tender to furious in about two seconds. "No." She stood directly in front of him and put her hands on her hips. She stood as tall as possible to get right in his face. He would have found it amusing if it didn't turn him on a little.

She struggled to find her words. "You will *not* take my property to the Council."

"I have an obligation to protect every being in this region. From what your English friend said, that trinket can cause major damage. It needs to be in the hands of someone who understands its power."

"No."

Mi-ma got back to her feet. "Come on, ladies. It's time to let Nell and Trent work things out." Sonja started to object but held her tongue with a look from Mi-Ma, and she and Trina followed the old Demon upstairs with no more hesitation.

Nell stood her ground. Trent didn't like the look in her eyes. She was going to fight him tooth and nail for this. Maybe she needed to.

"Nell, I need to take this. I need to let the Council have control over it. You know it too. That thing is why you got attacked. That thing is responsible for I don't know how many deaths."

She turned and yanked up the box. She slammed it shut and placed her palm over the center moth with the diamond. There was a swooshing sound as the moths took flight off the box, all of them. Golden wings fluttered and struggled into flight in the basement, the delicate creatures turning darker the farther they got from the spelled box in Nell's hand. One by one the Black Witch moths disappeared into the night through the broken basement window.

Nell stomped past him and up the stairs.

* * * * *

Nell stood on the porch clutching the box. Dark energy swirled around it, making her fingers feel as though they had been submerged in warm pudding. She pushed it away from her body. What was she going to do with it? Trent was correct in that it was a dangerous talisman. She couldn't very well keep it here. If it was so powerful that people wanted to kill for it, she wondered how it had come into her father's possession. Her family could sure use the money if it was *that* valuable. She needed help.

She felt Trent's presence as he approached. She seemed more in tune to his energy than usual. *That can't be good*, she thought.

"You're taking this from me anyway, aren't you?" she asked without turning to look at his face. She felt vulnerable all of a sudden. She looked at the box. Maybe the darkness of the blood magic was working on her.

"It needs to go to the Council. It's dangerous."

She turned. His hair was tussled and wild. Those blue eyes were pleading. Nell felt her resolve crumbling around her.

He stepped closer. Close enough she could feel the heat of his body. She looked at his chest to avoid his eyes. She knew his point was valid. The box and its contents were too much bad magic for her to handle. She inched closer to him.

"I need to take the box, Nell." His voice was low and gravely.

Nell swallowed hard and glanced up. The little scar on his left cheek twitched as he licked his lips. She wanted to kiss him. She wanted to strip him down, lay him on the deck and make all this go away. She looked him in the eye. He wanted it too. She licked her own lips without thinking about it.

Nell watched the slow closing of his eyes, the muscles of his jaw tighten, and felt his body stiffen. He was about to clam up, to pull away. She felt it. Damn. There had to be a way to break through to him, to help him understand that *he* controlled his future. The past he feared wasn't even *his* past. His grandfather and his father had made mistakes. That didn't mean Trent was going to.

"I'm taking it to New Orleans tomorrow. The Council is meeting there on other business."

She looked back out into the woods. "Trent. I need to know more about this thing. The Council can wait a few days, don't you think?"

"I can't. Too risky. What do you hope to accomplish? I'll take it to them, find out what the story is and let you know."

"I don't trust them. I never really have." Her voice was beginning to quiver in anger. She needed to be a part of this. If she let the box go, Trent might not come back. He'd tried so hard over the years to stay away from her. "They won't tell you anything they don't want to tell you. This box has to be worth a fortune. It was in my father's things."

He sighed, turning back to her. "What do you want me to do here, Nell?"

She wanted him to want to be with her. "Take me with you."

His head dropped. She dragged in a deep breath. "I'll be there to hear what they say. I can at least plead my case. You get to turn it in and protect me all at the same time. Everybody's happy."

"That won't help our situation."

He still wasn't looking at her. She wondered exactly which situation he was talking about? The "we're basically mated but can't be together" situation, or the "box with the deadly blood-magic gris-gris" situation?

He continued. "They're not going to let you have a say in what happens to it." He stepped off the deck. Nell followed and scooped up a handful of pebbles and mud and slung them at his back. He spun around, his mouth open in surprise.

"I'm going." Nell didn't back down.

"No. You're not."

"I'll follow you." His shoulders fell once again as he wiped the mud off one of them, flinging it back toward her. "Besides, you have to protect me. That creepy guy won't know you have the box and he'll still come after me." *Ha!* She had him there.

Trent shook his head and turned to the house. "Crazy-assed Demon," he mumbled as he moved away from her. "I may not kill *you*, but I have a feeling you'll be the death of *me*."

Chapter Nine

ஐ

"St. Louis number one," Trent said as the pair crawled into the minivan taking them into the French Quarter.

The taxi driver looked at his watch. "Cemetery closed at three."

He knew this bit of information. It would be fully dark by the time the cabbie got them there and the Council would be waiting. He wanted to get this over with and get away from Nell and his intense lust. He needed some space to work all this out.

He wished he could use his position as Prime to his advantage and request a transfer while he was here. Halfway around the world should do it. Too bad his pack was right across the gorge from Nell. He wondered how his pack members felt about China.

Trent had made it through most of last night by staying outside in his wolf form. The plane was managed by booking their seats at opposite ends of the aircraft. Now they had to make a short cab trip, get to the Council meeting and then he could walk away.

Nell sat beside him on the middle seat of the van. She looked up from studying the burn to her palm. Trina had been right. She was branded with the outline of the moth. Nell smiled at the driver. "No worries. We just want a few pictures. Short trip." She pulled out a piece of paper with notes scribbled on it. "Lots to see." The poor attempt at a cover was cute.

The cabbie shook his head.

As planned, it was dark as they pulled up to the gate on Basin Street. Trent paid the driver and pulled his pack out of the van. He felt the off-ness of the box inside like a descending dark cloud.

Nell hoisted her own backpack over her shoulders. "Now what?"

Trent headed to the right. Nell followed. "Don't you think they could have picked a location that was a little less populated? These cemeteries are usually playgrounds for teenagers at night. Aren't they?"

"The Council isn't concerned. And they rotate meeting locations. They seem to get a perverse thrill out of hiding in plain sight."

He tried to avoid coming before the Council as much as he could. Never liked being around that many beings with so much power. He turned up St. Louis Street, stopping about halfway down the brick and stucco wall that surrounded the cemetery. He leaned against the wall to watch the traffic pattern for a moment.

Nell looked around. "Are they all so public?"

"Just the entrance is public. But the locations do seem to have a strange sense of the ironic." He threw his pack over the wall. It landed with a thud that made Trent worry the box might have been damaged. He grabbed Nell's backpack and did the same. The light changed and the cars stopped again, and Trent leaned back against the wall.

"Ironic? Meaning?" She seemed antsy, pacing a small area just in front of him on the sidewalk.

"Cemeteries, old castles, famous haunted houses."

"Are they *trying* to be discovered?" She ran her fingers through her hair.

The light changed again. It was time. He cupped his hands and gestured for her. "Come on. I'll boost. Now. While there's no traffic."

She put her foot in his hands and he heaved her up. She easily topped the six-foot wall and disappeared to the other side. He looked up and down the street to make sure it was still clear before leaping up, catching the wall and pulling himself over.

She was putting her pack on as he jumped down from the wall. He grabbed his pack and flung it over one shoulder.

"This way." Trent grabbed her hand and headed down the crooked path that led between the unusual aboveground tombs. The place gave him the creeps and that box and its hinky Voodoo had his hair standing on end. They made a right and then a left. The tombs all looked the same to him.

He needed to find the wall of vaults that separated the Catholic tombs from the traditional Presbyterian graves. He knew it was near the back of the cemetery. He heard a noise and stopped.

"Isn't this Marie Laveau's tomb?"

"Shhh." He didn't like the idea of being right next to the Voodoo Queen's tomb with such a powerful gris-gris in his pack. He could make out all the Xs left on her tomb, requests for favors. He felt the power of the box reacting to the tomb through the nylon of the backpack.

And he felt someone close by. Others could feel this thing's power as well. "Shit."

There were lots of rumors about how dangerous New Orleans cemeteries were at night. The two times Trent had been here, he'd been aware of the possibility of rogue Vamps hanging out, but he'd been alone and not so worried about them or anything else hanging around a haunted cemetery in the dark.

"I don't like this," Nell whispered and placed her other hand on his upper arm. A Black Witch moth appeared out of nowhere and fluttered around her head.

He remembered what Trina had said about them being harbingers of death. Trent tightened his grip on her hand. "Follow and be ready to run."

They headed off to their right. The tombs of the dead were like miniature buildings, some soaring high above his head, some reduced to little more than broken bricks and rubble on the ground. He followed his instincts, heading deeper into the cemetery.

After one more turn he spotted the wall of decaying vaults that housed the entrance to an underground system, which would take them to the Council. It was at the end of a row of some renovated tombs that gleamed bright white in the moonlight. They were close, but the feeling of being watched had grown until Trent felt a pressing need to run, to protect Nell. The evil magic of the box was burning into his back.

As far as he was concerned right now, the sooner he could deposit that thing into the hands of the Council and get Nell out of here, the better. He hesitated as they passed each of the white, stucco-covered tombs. Anything could be hiding between them. And in this place, that really meant *anything*.

Nell stumbled and let go of his hand. He turned to check on her. "Okay?"

She nodded. He heard the rustle of movement to his right too late to react. "Run!" he ordered. He swung his arm toward the movement before he could fully shift, but knew he'd made contact — his last thought before he felt an impact to his head.

* * * * *

Nell saw Trent's head snap to the side as something appeared from nowhere and slammed into him. She stepped toward him but was yanked back by an arm that reached around and grabbed her from behind. A foul-smelling cloth was pressed against her mouth. Nell slammed her heel into the shin of her attacker, who stumbled and let go. She whirled to face him and realized the attackers were Vamps. Thin, starving Vamps. She closed her eyes and let her fear and anger push her shift.

It hurt as her Dragon emerged. Her skin stretched and changed swiftly. The bones in her hands and legs popped as they altered slightly. Only gaining about three inches in height and several pounds in girth wasn't going to help her much against feral Vamps, but it was all she had.

Her eyes opened to clearer night vision. Her mouth stretched and her teeth scraped together as her canines enlarged. The grinding sound made her shiver every time. She roared her anger at seeing Trent on the ground.

Her would-be captor hissed and showed his fangs. He was skinny and his face looked hollow, his eyes an eerie, milky white. His gums had receded, making the fangs look even more freakish. These weren't the same caliber of high-class Vamps she'd know and loved in Paris. The one facing her fit the desolate feel of the creepy tombs in the cemetery.

She stepped back and hissed as well. The Vamp charged. She stood her ground to fight, needing to stay with Trent and protect the box. The Vamp crashed into her with all the strength he could muster but her Demon form was stronger and sturdier. She swung and managed to connect her forearm to his temple. He stumbled slightly but came right back, slamming into her and knocking her aside several feet.

From the corner of her eye, she saw a female Vamp taking off with Trent's pack.

The box.

Her human mind fought for control. Her Dragon was pure, primal instinct. Her Demon *wanted*. It wanted to destroy the Vamp in front of her. She needed both the instinctual battle sense of her Demon and the intellect of her human side. They never played well together. She just needed enough control to change direction, to shift her attention to chase after the girl. It was like trying to rein in an entirely separate being who didn't want to be controlled.

The Vamp she'd been fighting lunged at her, trying to sink those ugly fangs into her neck. Nell swiped at him with a clumsy but potent swing. Her fingers, with their thin, sharp nails, struck his face and sliced it from eyebrow to chin. For a moment she wanted to taste the blood that oozed from his torn face. She wanted the spoils of victory.

The skinny Vamp swiftly crawled away from her, scurrying like a rat, disappearing between two of the tombs. She bit her lip, tasting her own essence to take the edge off the urge for blood. She braced herself against the nearest tomb, pressing her head to the stucco to fight for the coherent thought she felt slipping away. She smelled the decay of the body inside the tomb. Pulling her head away, she took a deep breath to try to reverse her shift but it was no use. Adrenaline was in control of her body at the moment and her Demon was content with that.

From the looks of it, Trent was out cold. She was afraid to get too close to him. What if she lost what little control she had over her urges? Goddess only knew what her Demon would do if it were close to an injured Trent Nicholas. Save him, fuck him? In his injured state, she might have the urge to take a big ol' bite out of his hide. She didn't know what her Demon would do, but whatever it was, it wouldn't be helpful.

It was up to her to recover the box. She took two large breaths. The easiest thing to do was go with her Demon, let it chase. She would deal with the aftermath if she caught the Vamp. She followed the path the girl had taken. Her feet beat hard on the graveled walkway. She sniffed. The air was hot and thick with Louisiana humidity.

The Vamps smelled of old meat, which made them easy to track. Nell caught up to her near the front of the cemetery. She wasn't moving very fast. Judging by the huge gash Nell spotted on her side, Trent got in one good blow. The Vamp spun on Nell, fangs showing, but her hiss was halfhearted. The pathetic thing wavered in her stance as if drunk. She looked tired, her face far too young. Maybe too young to have been turned.

Nell felt a wave of empathy. *Crap.*

The surge of emotion brought on an instant shift. No intention. It was a natural reaction that was part of the Halfling curse. Little control over the Demon. *Shit.*

She found herself face-to-face with a starving, threatened Vamp, in her much-weaker human form. The girl lunged forward. Her attempt to attack was as pathetic as Nell felt at present. With no effort, Nell dodged out of the way and the Vamp rushed past her and ran shoulder-first into a tomb.

The withering Vamp grunted as she tried to regain her balance. With what strength the girl could muster, she flung herself at Nell, this time falling against her, bear-hugging Nell and hanging off her like a worn-out boxer. She was light and bony in Nell's arms. She held her aloft, trying to lift the Vamp back to her feet.

Struggling to even to raise her head, the Vamp hissed again. Nell chuckled in amusement. The insult bolstered the girl, who mustered a bit of energy and struck at Nell like a snake, grabbing her shoulders and snapping at her neck. Nell's own arms trembled with weakness.

Nell concentrated and managed to summon what little *she* had left to thrust with her Demon power. Bricks from a nearby crumbling tomb flew straight up. Not what she had intended. There was no control over the speed or direction of the flying blocks.

What goes up, must come down—and come down it did. A shower of bricks and mortar rained down on the two of them.

A large brick crashed hard on the Vamp's back. She squealed and tried to turn her face away, letting go of Nell. Another connected with the crown of her head. Nell stumbled backward, only taking a hit to the leg as debris fell. The Vamp dropped the pack in an attempt to protect herself. She made tortured keening sounds as she stumbled backward.

The reeling, emaciated Vamp tripped on loose gravel and momentum carried her to the ground. She slammed onto her back. Her head made a loud cracking sound as it connected with the edge of one of the tombs. Gargling noises escaped her throat as her eyes closed.

Nell stood still, listening, letting her body settle from the changes and the thrust of telekinetic power. Her breathing slowed as she concentrated on calming down.

Her hands and knees hurt from the stretching and twisting of her skin and bones. Her shift was subtle, but it was still a shift. She clenched her fist to soothe the sore muscles. Dried blood dirtied her fingernails. She turned her head to each side to stretch her neck. The Vamp still lay unconscious. Good thing it was starving. Nell wouldn't have had a chance against a Vamp otherwise.

Everything was quiet. Too quiet. The pack lay by the Vamp's side.

Nell took two small steps toward the Vamp, prepared for the possibility of the creature playing possum. She nudged her with her foot. Nothing. The Vamp was out cold. She'd survive if someone came along and shared blood with her, but she was a bag of bones for the time being. Nell grabbed the pack. The Council could clean up this mess.

Convinced she was still not alone, Nell moved from tomb to tomb, sticking close to the darkened shadows. The button had popped off her shorts when she'd shifted and she held them closed as she headed back toward Trent, being cautious in case the male Vamp was lurking around the city of tombs. Hopefully Trent was looking for her by now.

The tombs looked like little spooky haunted houses in the moonlight. She heard shuffling noises and crouched in a shadow beside one of the big community tombs. The noises got louder but she couldn't see what it was. She moved through the rows until she finally caught a glimpse of two men ushering an unconscious Trent toward the front gate. They looked much healthier than the sickly Vamps who'd attacked them. Nell couldn't take the chance. If they were Vamps, she had no more power to fight their strength. If they were Weres, well…she was still as weak as a kitten right now. All she could do was follow.

One of them broke through the chain that held the front gate closed and they headed down a side street. Trent's arms hung limply over their shoulders as they carried him like a drunken friend. Nell had to hang back to prevent being seen. After two blocks, loud music drifted into the night. They were taking Trent into the heart of the French Quarter. She needed to catch up before she lost them in the crowds milling about, celebrating and drinking hurricanes.

She lurked in recessed doorways and alleys, trying to stay within a block of the trio. As soon as they turned onto Bourbon Street, Nell ran. If she lost them now she was in trouble. Far too many alleys and courtyards existed in this city.

Once she got to the corner, she could pick out the threesome only a half-block up. The revelers would work to her advantage now. She moved through the crowd of diverse tourists with relative ease.

The men maneuvered Trent around groups of tourists stopped in the middle of the street to drink or catch beads tossed from the balconies and galleries that lined Bourbon. There was a particularly large crowd of young men gathered outside one of the cathouses. A dark-skinned stripper stood on the sidewalk outside a bar called the Cat's Meow. Her bright pink g-string and itty-bitty bikini top left little to the imagination. The shapely woman turned her back to them and shook her ass in a jiggling invitation to come in and see the rest.

One of the spectators stepped back, directly into Nell's path. Since they were both watching the stripper instead of where they were going, they collided. The force of it made Nell falter and the pack slid off her shoulder. He managed to catch her and keep their collective balance.

Still holding her shorts closed, Nell tried to keep a grip on the pack. The reveler attempted to help her slide the pack back over her shoulder and Nell clutched it protectively. The guy backed up a step. "Sorry, babe," he said, and then his face flushed when he looked back at the stripper and realized Nell knew the cause of his clumsiness.

Nell nodded and pulled away, gripping the pack. The trio was still heading off down Bourbon Street. She barely saw them duck behind a hotdog cart and rushed to catch up.

When she reached the corner, they were nowhere to be seen.

She spun back to the busy street, scanning in case she'd been mistaken. No sign of them. She headed down St. Anne, looking through cracks in the large gates that hid courtyard gardens and alleyways. She hurried down the three blocks to Jackson Square. She circled around a large group of tourists waiting to go on a Vampire tour of the city. If they only knew.

She'd lost them.

The sensation of panic and loss rushed through her body like a surge of adrenaline. She clenched her fist, feeling the burn of the moth's brand, and started back up the street. If something happened to Trent, she didn't know what she'd do. The thought of losing him made her stomach hurt.

Exhausted, she sat on a bench in front of the huge Catholic church that overlooked Jackson Square. Two men were playing a sad jazz melody on trumpets a dozen or so feet away. Nell suddenly felt very alone.

She needed help. The Council was her best choice. Right now she'd gladly turn the box over to them if they'd help her find Trent, but she knew she'd never find the secret entrance to the clandestine meeting place on her own. She opened Trent's pack, searching for a clue. She reached beneath the wooden box that was the cause of all this trouble, hating the sickening feel of the blood magic it contained.

She pulled out two t-shirts and some deodorant. Her own backpack had been lost in her change and fight with the Vamps. She fished deeper into the pack. His phone. She opened it, only to discover the screen asked for a password. Shit. She tried the very few things she thought might work—

his birthday, his name and the numbers of his street address. No luck. She pressed the numbers that corresponded to *her* name. Not surprisingly, that didn't work either. She tossed the phone back in the bag.

She leaned back and looked up into the darkness. Nothing left to do but follow the only other clue she had. The box. It held a Voodoo talisman and she was in a city rich with Voodoo history. Nell flung the pack over her shoulder and headed back in the direction she'd come.

The front gate of the cemetery was still busted open, the lock and chain useless on the sidewalk. She slipped in and headed back to where the attack had commenced. The feeling of being watched or that she wasn't alone was absent on this trip through.

Luckily, her pack had been left behind by the nasty Vamps. She fished inside the front pocket, relieved to find her wallet still there. At least she had a change of clothes and some money.

The wall of vaults that held the secret passage to the Council's meeting place looked to be exactly what it was—a thick, concrete wall full of tombs. Where Trent had been heading to find the passage, she had no clue. Bodies were left in these things for a year to deteriorate. No way was Nell going to try to open any of the vaults to check for tunnels. She followed the wall around to the backside. More brick and stucco. No indication of a door or passage.

Using her fist, she banged on a small, round area where the stucco was missing and the brick looked loose. The muffled noise wouldn't carry very far. "Hello?" she said aloud, but very low. She didn't want to attract any more attention of the Vampiric kind.

This is stupid, she thought. The Council wouldn't give a crap about Trent even if she *could* get in. All they'd want was the box and once they had it, Trent would be on his own. It was up to her to find him. Boy, he'd love that.

116

She exited the cemetery the way she and Trent had entered, over the wall, just in case there was someone back at the front gate waiting for her.

* * * * *

Sweat was running down the back of Nell's shirt as she sat at an iron table outside a closed café. The place was deep in an alley off the major streets of the Quarter, giving her some sense of safety. She fumbled with getting minutes on the pay-as-you-go phone she'd purchased from a corner grocery. She'd bought the phone, a bottle of water, some Cheetos and a soggy turkey sandwich wrapped in cellophane.

She ate half the sandwich and all the Cheetos. The oppressive feel of the dark magic was wearing on her, making her stomach queasy. She wiped sweat and dirt from her face with the Wet-Nap she'd gotten from the deli counter then changed her clothes so she didn't look like a street urchin.

She wondered about Trent as she combined the contents of both packs into one. Sorry she let the thought in, Nell imagined the worst—Trent dead and at the bottom of the Mississippi river. Closing her eyes and picturing him angry and chastising was much better. She needed to fix this. It was all her fault. She tossed the dirty shirt and damaged shorts in a trash bin on her way out of the alley. Time to move. And who she needed to find would be in a quieter part of the Quarter.

It had been years since she'd been here. She'd visited the city with a wicked-fun Sorcerer named Avery who had known the area and all its nonhuman inhabitants. That trip had been a party. Drinking and dancing with his coven, jazz music all night long in a back-alley courtyard. Waking up to cool breezes on the banks of the Mississippi river.

Nell trusted her instincts and let her internal compass lead her toward the river for a few blocks. The well-kept house fronts gave way to homes with bent, rusted wrought iron and broken boards. The smell of the dirty part of the city was getting thicker. The Quarter always held the most curious stench of rotting food and body odor.

Nell stopped under a streetlight. Soft jazz music filled the night air. It stopped and she heard voices and laughter and then the music picked up again. Late-night party in one of the courtyards.

She rounded the corner and saw what she was searching for. A small, black sign hung from the bottom of a very tilted balcony, its words long since worn away. The faint image of sticks and stones painted in dingy white on the bottom of the sign was enough to tell Nell she had found the right place.

The door was open, the shop itself deeply shadowed. A heavy drum rhythm drifted into the street from inside. A fat gray and white tabby lounged on the sidewalk, leaning on the bottom step leading inside the shop. The dirty furball didn't flinch as Nell stepped through the door.

"You's not bringin' that dark charm inta my place, is you?" The voice, heavy in Cajun accent, came from Nell's right. Darkness behind the counter veiled the speaker. The fact that the woman knew she had the damn thing doubly verified she'd found the right place. It also made her a bit nervous.

"I was hoping—"

"You was lookin' for someone to enlighten you?" The woman appeared from behind the counter as if materializing out of the night itself. Her bright yellow skirt swished against her legs in the low light. The brightness of it and her startling appearance made Nell blink. Something splattered on Nell's face. The shock made her retreat, stumbling down the steps and back onto the sidewalk. The cat hissed.

Nell wiped her face. Ash and who knew what else. She brushed it off on her thigh. The woman stood in the doorway, making it clear Nell was not to bring the pack or, more importantly, the necklace back into the building. The old, dark-skinned woman's face was wrinkled by time and hardship. Her skirt was tattered, the bottom hem torn, strings hanging loose and dirty. Her tight, red camisole shirt showed every bony curve of the tiny woman's ribs.

The woman lit a half-smoked cigar. "You." She jutted her chin out and tilted her head to study Nell. She pointed a crooked, boney finger at her. "You brought me that Chinese root when you's here last, you did?"

Nell huffed in surprise. She and Avery had come to see this woman and he'd brought a gift of some rare root. Nell couldn't remember what it was or why he'd brought the stuff. "My friend did, yes."

The woman plopped down on the highest of the three steps and tucked her skirt between her spread knees. "You got more now?" She let out a large puff of smoke that formed a perfect ring.

"I'm sorry. No." Nell thought through what she *did* have with her—a little makeup, deodorant, the newly acquired phone and the content's of Trent's backpack. "Werewolf hair."

"Ain't so rare 'round these parts, girly, but useful. Very useful." Another smoke ring floated in front of Nell's face.

"I just need you to look at something. See if you have any clue where it may have come from. Perhaps you'll know who might want it. I'll stay out here." Nell started to pull her pack off.

"Holy Jesus, chile!" She snubbed the cigar out on the step. The cat brushed against her leg on its way inside. "Not out here in front o' the Lord and everyones. Bugaboos for miles can feel that creepy mojo. Lucky girly to be alive this long. Come whid me." She got up and headed down the street, leaving the door to her shop open. Who steals from a Voodoo Queen? Talk about bad karma.

Nell followed for two blocks. The woman stopped by a high wooden fence. She fiddled with the lock on the gate then pushed it in. The gray and white tabby shot through the opening. They followed him through, down an alley into a gorgeous courtyard full of flowering plants and twinkling lights.

The old woman stopped and pointed, indicating Nell should sit. There were several tables with big green umbrellas, decorated with plants and brightly colored bowls. A fountain gurgled from an unseen location, probably tucked behind one of the large oleanders. Beautifully painted wood screens hid the plumbing and wiring that was outside most of the hundred-year-old homes in the French Quarter.

Nell sat at the closest table. The old Voodoo Queen walked away. Nell rummaged in the pack and pulled out Trent's shaving kit. From that, she retrieved his brush. Werewolf hair.

"*Your* hair most likely be of more interest." Again, Nell was startled by the seemingly ghostly appearance of the old woman. She sat at another table a few feet away from Nell and poked that chin out again. "What exactly is you?" she asked as the cat wound itself around her feet.

Nell stood as another, younger woman entered. She couldn't have been more than twenty, her skin a flawless, silky caramel color. She was dressed in bright green cotton pajamas.

"Hello."

Nell realized the woman's eyes were cloudy. She was blind. Although her face was young and her voice sweet, the woman's power billowed before her like a cloud. *This* was the Voodoo Queen. "Hi. My name is Nell Ambercroft. I'm trying to find a friend."

She gestured for Nell to sit again. "I am Barri." She took the seat next to Nell, turning the chair so they faced one another. "You mean your wolf?" Her fingers unerringly touched the brush in Nell's hand while her blank eyes remained on Nell's face.

"Yes. My wolf."

"And you need to know the power of the gris-gris you have in the magic box. You are not in a position that one

120

would envy, little Dragon." She lifted the hair off the back of her neck and twisted it into a bun on top of her head. "My aunt was correct; your hair is a far stronger ingredient for mojos than the simple wolf fur."

"How did you know?" Nell couldn't remember anyone ever deciphering her Demon's form without knowledge of her parentage or seeing her change.

"I see what others overlook." She held out her hand. Her palm was scarred with a thousand small cuts. "Place your left hand in mine."

Nell set the brush down and rested the pack between her feet. She looked at the old woman, who had relit her cigar and was now smiling knowingly at Nell. The cat had made his way onto the tabletop. His leg was hiked high and he was happily cleaning his balls without a care.

The old woman laughed as Nell placed her hand in Barri's. With the gentleness of a mother, she turned Nell's hand and traced the brand. It was no longer sore but she felt a little sting as Barri touched it.

Several moths gathered under the umbrella, their shadows flitting in the lights. "You're back," she said to the insects as one landed on her arm.

"The box is reacting to your magic, calling them, conjuring them." Barri tapped the brand. "You'll need them again if you want to open it."

"Are they even real?" Nell asked.

"They are as real as your power. As mine." Barri uttered something Nell didn't understand but her aunt got up and went behind a huge oleander bush. She returned quickly with an ornately carved, black-and-tan carafe and set it on the table.

"First," Barri said, placing her other hand on top of Nell's. "I will cleanse you of the evil in that puzzle box and see if I can quiet its call to the same. It wants companionship. Blood magic that strong calls to those who would use it. You are like a beacon in the night for the damned." She tilted her head as if to listen to the night itself. "New Orleans is not the city you want to be roaming about, calling out to evil. Place the box on the table, under our joined hands." Nell bent to retrieve the box from the pack. "But do not foul my skin with it, please."

Nell now wished she hadn't touched it either. She didn't like the thought of being fouled. Her sisters and Mi-ma were also fouled. She slid it beneath their clasped hands.

"Lavender oil, vodka and holy water." She carefully reached for the carafe with no fumbling. She dribbled the concoction over their hands and onto the box. "Shroud me in goodness and spiritual light. Dampen the darkness with power and might. Spirits which cling, you're not wanted inside."

Nell watched the box begin to vibrate and hum. It was brief. Then Nell felt it—a major lessening of that sick, dark feeling she'd been fighting all night.

"You should be safe from the bloodsuckers for a while." She stuck her thumb and index finger into a pouch that hung around her neck. "Dead Sea salt. To protect you." She sprinkled the pinch over Nell's hand.

"Thank you," Nell said.

"It will not stop the one who seeks it."

Again Nell was impressed. "You know his name?"

Barri tried to pull away. "Names hold power. You know that."

Nell understood her concern. She let go of the woman's frail hand. "You don't want to conjure him here?"

Barri smiled. The old woman cackled from behind them. "No, Nell Ambercroft. His is not the kind of energy I wish to visit my house. Yours, though…your energy is welcome."

"I see." Evidently her name wasn't high on the scary scale when it came to power. "My hair…"

The old woman had a tiny pair of scissors at the ready. Nell had no idea where she'd kept them, but it didn't matter.

She handed them to Barri. "Hold a lock from behind your left ear."

Nell followed her instructions and grasped a small bit of hair near the base of her head. Barri placed her hand on Nell's arm and used it to guide her to the end of Nell's fingers, stopping where Nell held the hair. With her other hand, she reached forward and snipped the lock, using Nell's fingers as an indicator of where to cut.

"Golden Dragon," Barri said, her hand still resting on Nell's arm, "can heal turmoil of the mind. In this city, it is much needed these days."

Even blind, Barri saw more than most. "Take more." Nell grabbed another section of hair. She had tons of it. If it would help someone else, she was happy to donate.

Barri cut again then patted Nell's arm. Then she spoke to the old woman. Nell was sure it was English but the Cajun dialect was far too fast and heavy for her to make out.

"Follow Auntie. My cousin has an empty apartment he is trying to rent. Stay there during the daylight hours. Rest. Eat. At dusk, take a cab out of the city to the bayou, the Airboat Adventures dock. Ask for Cap'n Allen. He'll be waiting. He'll know where your wolf is."

"Thank you. Again." The old woman was heading for the street before Nell could gather her pack. Nell looked Barri in the eyes and nodded again in thanks, sure she felt it even if she couldn't see it. She then rushed to catch up with the barefoot old woman and followed her back into the hot streets of the French Quarter.

Chapter Ten

∞

The smell of diesel fuel and swamp rot filled the air as she stepped from the cab. Nell looked out over the sunset. Bright orange and pink highlighted the dull aluminum of the few boats tied to the long dock. There was a large metal building up the driveway, open bay doors revealing the skeletons of several more boats and the rusted-out remains of a Mustang. The ride had taken forty-five minutes and a hundred-dollar bill. Once the cab left, Nell was alone in the middle of nowhere.

Nell crossed the gravel parking lot and lightly tapped on the door of the tour boat office.

"They's closed for the night, miss." The voice didn't exactly startle her, but she was sure no one had been down by the airboats when she got out of the cab. Now a large, white-haired man was behind her.

"Captain Allen?" Nell took a step toward the big man. He tilted his head in question. "Barri said you might help me."

"Madame Barri said that, did she?" He scratched the side of his head with dirty fingernails then dug in the deep pocket of his camouflage pants. "I ain't got a call from her in months."

He flipped open the cell phone that looked way too small in his thick fingers. "Oops. Reckon I did." He pushed a couple buttons and listened. He shook his head as he closed the phone.

Nell waited to hear if that message pertained to her or not. She stood still and attempted not to show how anxious she was over this entire situation.

Without commentary, he headed toward the dock. "You want to go out there at night, I'll take ya's." He stopped suddenly and turned back to Nell. Even several feet away she was closer to him than she would have liked. He was tall and thick and smelled of dead fish. "I ain't going all the way in though. I'll take you to Naked Creek." He sniffed the air.

Nell decided it was time to speak. "I have no idea what that means. I have a missing friend."

"I know what you lost, miss. If he's where I think he is, you may not want him back. Lots of folks goes out there and they never gets back." He continued toward the airboat at the end of the dock. "I knows that's mostly hearsay and Voodoo mumbo shit, but I've lived in these swamps all my life and found no cause to test out them rumors myself." He climbed aboard and held out a meaty hand to assist Nell off the dock and onto the rocking boat deck. "Got to be an old codger that way. And I aim to make it to old fuck someday."

He winked. Nell nodded her head. "I'd like that myself."

"You got any weapons in that bag, miss?"

Nell shook her head.

"Might oughta have one." The boat was little more than an aluminum platform with shallow sides. He opened a storage area in the front of the boat and Nell made note there were lifejackets in case she needed one. He moved some stuff she couldn't name the purpose of to one side and came up with a large machete in a leather case. "This'll take the head off most anything. From them rumors and what Madame Barri said, you'll likely need to do just that, miss. Whatever you find out there, take its head off, ya hear?" He handed her a large set of yellow earmuffs. "It's gonna get loud when that fan gets going."

Nell looked at the giant fan mounted on the back of the boat. The captain's chair was mounted right in front of it. There was a seat to each side of his and a bench in front of that, which would hold three more passengers. "Not sneaking up then?"

He pointed to one of the seats next to his and then gave her a big, toothy smile. "Don't you's worry, miss. Once we get out there, I'll guide us in nice and quiet like." He sat in his chair. "I can sneak up on a mating gator and steal his girl before he knowed it."

He flipped the switch on the ignition and the fan roared to life. "You might oughta sit now, miss." Nell noticed there were no seat belts.

The sun was tucking behind the cypress trees as they hit open water that Nell suspected was a lake. He pointed to his earmuffs and indicated she do the same. When he pushed a large lever forward, the fan went full blast and the airboat took off as if flying over the calm, black water. It was as exhilarating as it was frightening.

For several minutes it seemed they headed straight to the middle of a very large lake. The sun had completely set, leaving only the smallest trace of a burnt-orange glow across the sky. Nell had no sense of scale to judge the distance they had traveled before he veered off to the left.

In the dark, he careened through the canals and narrow tributaries that made up the swamps. Nell gripped the edge of her chair. Even with her good night vision, she could barely make out the contrast of dark water against the even darker vegetation along the banks. Captain Allen knew where he was going. He switched the direction of the boat on a dime and flung them, sailing sideways just as much as forward, into what looked like a cove.

He yanked off his ear protection. Nell removed her own as he shut off the engines and hopped to the floor of the boat. They drifted to a stop.

"Yeeee woooo, Miss Blonde!" he barked into the night sky. "That there was a purty night ride."

Nell couldn't help enjoying the adrenaline rush that accompanied the scare. "That it was, Captain." She shook her head. She'd thought she'd been on adventures during her travels. But she'd been living a tourist's life. Spas and a gondola ride in Venice were an outright snore compared to this. Trent would have loved it.

She looked around the cove. She had business to attend to. She needed to get her head back on the task at hand. "So um...what now?"

"Now..." He started rowing toward some pipes sticking up out of the water in the middle of the cove. A small johnboat was tied to what looked to be some sort of piping for an oilrig. "You, miss, is gonna take your own night ride."

"Great," Nell muttered, noticing how close to the gator-infested waters that tiny boat would leave her.

He pulled the airboat alongside the smaller boat and tossed her pack in. Then he set the machete on top of it. He handed her a flashlight. "Only use it when you have to. No telling what you'll attract out there in the dark."

Nell nodded, not really wanting to ask. She imagined all kinds of huge flying bugs landing in her hair, and shivered. The moths would be welcome at this moment.

"Step on in and get settled in the middle."

"You're not going to try to talk me out of heading out there?"

"If'n you've been to Madame Barri already and she's sending you out here, I reckon you're in as good a spot as any to go. She sees. I ain't abouts to question her intentions." He fished around in the storage bin again and handed Nell a big bag of marshmallows.

She raised her brows. "What are the those for?"

"The gators love 'em. If you get in a spot where you're cornered, toss 'em. In the water or out."

She put them on the floor of the boat by her feet. "Marshmallows?"

He shrugged. "We been using 'em for years to bring gators to the tour boats." He leaned in closer, resting his big hands on his knees. "You head to your right out the opening of this here cove. Stay close to the middle of the big channel. Use what little current is there. Pass three backwaters and head inta the fourth."

"Backwaters?" Nell asked as she gripped the oar and looked at the trees behind the captain. Spanish moss hung low off the branches over the water. Snakes probably liked this place a lot.

"Inlets. Tributaries." Nell nodded her understanding and he continued. "It'll be on the left. It gets real narrow like in there. The moss'll be hanging low and it'll look like you can't make it out the back, but you can. Follow it round to the second one on the right."

Nell repeated the combination. "Go right, four then left. Two then right?"

"That's it. After that, I know nothing. I hears there is several shotgun shacks where they make shine. Everything else I hears, I ain't sharing with you."

Nell took a deep breath as he pushed her off, shoving the johnboat toward the opening to the cove. She lifted the oar and started to row.

"I'll be here 'til morning." His loud voice echoed off the black water. "You get your friend and get his ass back here, I'll get you out."

Nell looked back over her shoulder, taking care not to rock the little boat. "You're waiting?"

"I was gonna be fishing for the night anyways. Here's as good as any. You ain't back by morning, I'm gonna consider you a ghost." He shook his head.

As she rounded the corner of the main canal and lost sight of Captain Allen, she was somewhat comforted by the knowledge the old codger was waiting.

The quiet was interrupted with the wild call of a bird she suspected was a night heron. The sounds of her oar hitting the water seemed to echo loudly along the channel. She heard a splash, and then another. She closed her eyes and tried to think of something other than twenty-foot alligators. It was hard.

She recalled the other morning with Trent, how he'd been tender and loving. If she managed to get him out of this situation, she just might kill the stubborn bastard.

* * * * *

Flames. Blood. Graves. Trent's thoughts were scattered. His head hurt. He couldn't stretch his body, couldn't open his eyes to make the crazy dreams go away. He heard a thumping, rhythmic and steady hammering. It hurt his ears. Tired. So tired.

He took several shallow breaths. He must be sick. Really sick. He tried to concentrate. When that hurt his head too much, he tried to relax. Tried to stop fighting the numb feeling stealing over his mind. When that was gone, he'd ask Nell what they'd eaten on the plane.

Nell.

A flash of memory seared his brain. Nell, shifted as much as her Halfling body could shift, charging a Vampire. Pain. Black. Smoke.

She can't protect herself, he shouted in his mind. He wanted to move. Needed to find her. Why was he so weak? His eyes wouldn't open.

A voice spoke on the edge of his understanding, but it was muffled, reverberating in his head. Trent tried to take a deep breath, his chest burning with the effort.

His wrists started to sting—they were tied. So were his legs.

"…no use." Someone was talking to him. Trent tried to open his eyes again. This time they cracked a bit, fuzzy images, bright yellow light.

"Struggling's only going to hurt you worse, stupid dog."

That he understood. *Male voice. Not friendly.*

He closed his eyes again and tried to take in another deep breath. The thumping was a blasting echo of his own heartbeat and it was speeding up. Trent tried to center his energy. His wolf wanted to leap, to tear, but until he assessed the situation, that wasn't a viable option.

"That's it. Calm yourself. Don't want you to blow a gasket." The voice was annoyingly sharp.

The smell of burnt meat overwhelmed Trent's senses. His wolf forced open his eyes. Things were a bit clearer. A skinny arm held a piece of meat right in front of Trent's face. Cat. Trent turned away from it.

"Aw. And I hunted that thing down just for you. Don't be so ungrateful." Trent's vision refocused on the hollow face of the man crouched beside him. The bastard looked as if he'd been beaten more than once in his life. He had a scar from the side of his nose to the corner of his mouth. Another one over his right eye, about two inches long. He was missing a few teeth and his nose had been broken at least a couple of times.

He shoved the meat toward Trent's closed mouth. Trent turned his head away again.

"All right. So much for me trying to be hospitable and all. Have it your way. Just thought you might like a last meal."

Again Trent tried to stretch but with his hands tied behind his back and around some sort of post, which seemed to be in the middle of a small room, his movements were vastly limited. His head was pounding more than ever.

"Don't suppose you have any aspirin?" Trent figured this was Crey.

The Sorcerer laughed out loud. "Look around you, Prime. We got nothing but fire," he patted the handgun tucked in this belt, "and fire power. Not shit for supplies out here. I really gotta talk to my business associates. You'd think they'd have some food or something for me, with what I paid." He spit on the dirty wood plank floor.

Trent glanced around the room as his senses slowly returned and the pounding in his head subsided to a manageable rumble. It was a shack. Wood plank walls surrounded him. Four straight-back pine chairs and a lopsided table stood in one corner. The other side of the room had a series of unlevel shelves. The top three were empty. The bottom one held a stack of dust-covered magazines. There was a large jug next to the door, which was constructed of three boards fastened together with two smaller perpendicular slats.

The sounds of the night entered through the cracks between the boards of the walls. He heard the call of a heron and frogs singing happily from the shore, ready to plunge into the water at the first sign of a predator. Trent had a good idea where they were. Not good at all.

He stretched his head to the side to relieve some cramping. How long had he been here? "Not exactly the Four Seasons is it?"

The creepy Crey snorted out a laugh. "No, man. It's not." He offered the cat meat a third time. Trent still refused. "Not to worry. We won't have to endure these accommodations for much longer."

"Oh?" Trent was testing his bonds. Wire, and it was tight; no breaking through that no matter how much of his strength he got back.

"You have something I need." The little man smiled.

As Crey straightened and moved to look out a small window adjacent to the door, Trent saw the pyre. "Fuck."

A few amulets were scattered next to the fire. Trent felt the blood magic. The two-bit Sorcerer must have been stealing spells and power amulets to boost his power. That's how he'd spelled the human at Nell's house. That's how Trent's shift was being blocked now.

Crey turned back to Trent. "You know what that means, do ya?" He shoved another piece of meat in this mouth and didn't bother to wait until he was finished chewing to continue. "You're in deep kimchi, my furry friend."

Trent struggled against his bonds one more time because he didn't know what else to do at the moment.

"Easy there, Prime. I can jack it back up." He gestured to the pile of crap smoldering on the floor. "The spell. If need be. I wanted you conscious."

He squatted down to Trent's eye level once more and propped his elbows on his bent knees. "I want to know what you and the Halfling did with the box. Her old man shouldn't have kept such powerful toys." He shook his head.

"Where's Nell?" Trent looked the little scumbag in the eye.

"That's what I want to know, dude. My hired help didn't follow instructions very well. They were supposed to bring the girl and the box." He poked Trent in the chest a couple of times then stood and scratched his crotch. "Instead, the methhead vamps brought you."

Crey took another bite of the cat meat. "My boss wants the box but I got other plans. That necklace is gonna set me free, dog. Bye-bye slave, hello master status. Tell me where to find it and we all go home happy."

Trent laughed. "How stupid do I look?"

"Stupid enough to lose your girlfriend and the talisman all at the same time." He winked at Trent. "Don't worry, dude. I'll take real good care of your girl." He wriggled his nonexistent eyebrows.

Trent roared with anger. He tried to shift, to let his snout elongate, show some teeth, but agonizing pain shot though his body. Pain stronger than any he'd ever felt. He screamed, his entire body tightening. His eyes watered, mucus dripped from his searing nose. He slumped to the side, shivering. With his hands tied around the post, his shoulders were wrenched when he sagged toward the floor, arms stretched at an awkward angle. Dirt clung to his face.

"Dude. That looked like it really, really hurt. I suggest you not try that shit again."

Trent couldn't see the little bastard but he heard the amusement in his voice. He tried to steady his erratic breathing. He had to calm down. Nell was going to need him to keep his wits. He was now bait.

And Nell would take it. He knew it with all his heart. No way had she taken the box and found a way to contact the Council. She was just crazy enough to think she could rescue him.

And it was *his* fault she'd feel desperate enough to do it. She'd waited too long, hoped for too long. And he'd let her down. He'd hurt her over and over again by trying to stay out of her life. Why? So he could lose her this way?

The thought of anything happening to her made his stomach turn. This little freak was *not* going to touch her. She was *his*.

If anyone was going to kill Nell, it would be Trent.

He shook his head and laughed at his own thoughts. The irony.

"You think it's funny, Prime?" Crey asked.

Trent opened his eyes. Crey was sitting in one of the chairs at the table. He studied the little creep. Nothing was going to happen here. This creep would need to take Trent back to the city to lure Nell into a trap. Trent would use that opportunity to make his move. In the meantime, he needed to figure out how to break the spell.

He tried to right himself again. "I think you're right. I think that shit hurt."

Chapter Eleven

🔊

Nell found the backwater. The moon was bright and she could see that the forest had been carved out just enough to accommodate three small shacks. Surrounded by trees on all sides, probably barely visible from the water for an average human, the shacks sat a short distance back from the shoreline. Light was coming though the cracks of the closest tiny hut and she smelled burning hair. Not good. She maneuvered the boat to the little dock in front of the farthest shack. The metal hull hitting the wood post of the dock made a louder noise than she would have liked. A larger boat with a small motor was already tied up at the first dock, facing away from the shore. With any luck, she'd be leaving in that one.

With the machete in hand and the pack on her back, she tiptoed out of the boat, making her way to the shack along the line of trees that abutted the water. The sounds of the forest had died at her presence. She stood still among the tall cypress trees for a moment to allow nature to grow accustomed to her. The frogs started singing a few at a time. The rest of the swamp sounds, which Nell imagined came from all manner of slimy bugs and creatures, chimed in a few minutes later.

She felt secure in her stealth for the moment. She crouched, taking small steps to make her way to the back of the hut. She knelt beneath a crude window and listened. She heard a voice that sounded more like that of a teenager than a man. Had she come to the wrong backwater?

She inched up until she could just see over the ledge of the tiny window. The smell of blood magic made her stomach turn so violently she had to kneel back down. She took three large, cleansing breaths. Trent was in there. She'd managed to see him—or at least the back of him—as well as a man who was on a cell phone on the far side of the shack.

She unsnapped the machete sheath and pulled out the huge blade. It was clean and sharp. The voice was getting closer. The guy was pacing while talking on the phone, and heading her way. Nell hunched down farther and pressed herself up against the wall.

"I don't like it. I can't hold this spell forever." He cleared his throat.

Nell could hear a voice on the other end of the phone but couldn't understand the words.

Nell heard the phone snap shut. "Well, Prime, seems our ride has been delayed. Fuck. Finding last-minute help in this place is impossible."

"Pity," Trent replied. He sounded weak.

The little man cursed again. "I'm not so hot for your riveting conversation, Prime."

It was quiet for a moment. Nell wanted to look in again to get a feel for the layout. She was going to have to use her Demon gift, as much as she hated to. It was all she had. She heard chanting and a surge of light blasted through the window.

Nell rose quickly, using the blast of light to her advantage. The man was crouched over a little fire, casting a spell. Trent was writhing, his arms awkwardly tied around a post in the center of the room. The creepy-looking Sorcerer was seriously into his work. This was her chance.

The window was too small to get through quickly. As fast as she could, Nell ran back around to the door. Taking a deep breath to brace her resolve, she lunged forward, hitting the plank door with her shoulder.

It bounced her backward, not giving a bit.

So much for the element of surprise.

A gun fired and wood splintered. Nell screamed and dropped to the ground, almost losing hold of the machete. Terrified, she crawled back to the edge of the woods.

Everything was quiet. Nell's heart was pounding. That adrenaline rush she usually loved so much seemed annoying at the moment. She hadn't even considered a Sorcerer would have a gun. *Stupid girl.*

"Nell Ambercroft," the Sorcerer hollered out of the building. "How kind of you to come to us out here in the bayou. We were planning a reception for you in town. You've made this very easy for me." He cackled. "You bring that fucking necklace thingy in here and I'll let you and your boyfriend go."

Yeah right. She wasn't *that* stupid. She needed to buy some time. And how the hell did he know it was her?

She heard him cracking up at himself and worried over the fact that Trent hadn't weighed in on the conversation. For that matter, she was even more shocked he hadn't started cursing at her for being in the bayou in the first place. Way too uncharacteristic for the Were.

"Hee-hee-hee." The man's evil laugh chilled her spine. "Your boyfriend is a little, um, shall we say, under the influence right this minute. Evidently he can't hold his magic."

Nell needed to see if Trent was indeed okay after that spell. "Open the door. Let me see him and I'll bring the box." She pulled the backpack off her shoulders and held it out. She was tucked behind a cypress but Crey should be able to see the pack. The door opened all the way in.

It was less than a dozen feet from the tree line to the door. Nell eased out a little so she could see inside, machete hidden behind her leg.

In the middle of the tiny hut, she could see Crey standing over a bound Trent Nicholas, Super Werewolf, with a gun pointed at the Prime's head. She had no clue how she was going to get out of this situation.

"Um. I...uh. I need to go to the bathroom."

"What?" Crey looked at Trent. "Did she really say that?"

Trent's head lifted slightly. He looked as if he was heavily drugged. "Sounds right."

He was alive. Nell backed father into the woods. "I'll be right back."

The gun in Crey's hand wildly gestured toward Nell before she lost sight of him by tucking behind the large cypress again. "Is she serious?" he yelled. "Did she just take a potty break during a hostage negotiation?"

Nell didn't hear if Trent responded. She leaned against the tree, her mind racing for a plan. She'd seen what she'd needed to see. Treat was alive but out of commission. Crey had a gun. She had a machete. The odds were not in her favor.

Two small alligators moved away from the shore to her left, heading to the water.

Marshmallows...

Nell headed back to the boat, cringing each time she had to take a step. It was pitch black in the shadows of the cypress trees. Their huge roots stuck up out of the ground like the humps of sea monsters, slick and wet with the moisture of the swamp. Moss and bugs coated the branches she used for handholds as she steadied her balance, making her way to the boat as quietly as possible. Fortunately the creep holding Trent was too busy harping on and on about women to really notice her movement.

Nell got the bag of marshmallows and went back to the spot where the gators had slipped into the dark water. She tossed several in what she hoped was their general direction. One gator must have seen the movement as the treat landed because he went after it fast, gobbling it up. He opened his mouth and hissed at her as if to beg for more.

She tossed a few on the shore and then one even farther, into the trees. The second gator raced to get it before the first.

They clashed, hissing and knocking each other with their long snouts.

"Easy boys. I need you." She gathered the machete, the backpack and her energy. She only had one shot at this. She led the gators to the edge of the woods with a trail of marshmallows.

Nell stuffed a handful in her bra. Then she tossed the rest of the white, fluffy gator crack in the open area between the woods and the door of the hut. They only needed to get about six feet closer to the door. The gators rushed out of the woods in pursuit of the treats, hissing and charging toward the hut.

"Fucking bitch. Can the Halfling talk to animals?" He took a step back and aimed the gun at one of the gators.

Nell closed her eyes and pushed out with every bit of energy she could muster.

Gators went flying. One sailed past Crey, crashing into the wall behind him. The other smacked directly into his chest.

The gators were hissing in threat, Crey was cussing and Trent was laughing uncontrollably. Crey had dropped the gun to fend off the flying gator, allowing it to skitter over by the table.

Nell rushed in screaming and swung the machete in a large, chopping arc. It came down on Crey, cutting several inches into his shoulder.

The man roared and tried to back up, the machete still lodged in his shoulder right next to his neck. Nell didn't let go of the handle so she was pulled back with him. She yanked, trying to dislodge her weapon.

"Fucking Bitch!"

She pulled on the handle again as Crey tried to grab her arms. The gator closest flung his head toward the pair, not caring what the humans were fighting over. Nell pulled harder, desperate to swing the machete again.

She heard Trent growl. He was face-to-face with one of the gators, who still seemed pretty upset by his unscheduled flight. An agitated alligator was not a pretty alligator. Nell let go of the machete and grabbed some of the marshmallows she'd shoved down her shirt for safekeeping, tossing one close enough to Trent to get the gator's attention. He turned this toothy mouth to the treat and away from Trent. The other followed his buddy's lead. Nell tossed several more toward the door.

"Good thinking, baby," Trent said, sounding rather drunk. "I may have to give you a reward later for rescuing me." He raised his eyebrows in exaggerated insinuation. He was smiling, enjoying the show with no hint of fear or concern.

A crash brought Nell's attention back to Crey, who was trying to get the gun from under one of the chairs. When he bent over, the handle of the machete had connected with the table. He cursed loudly but was close to retrieving the weapon.

Nell had no shot at getting the gun or getting the machete back. She frantically searched for something to attack with. There wasn't shit left in the shack but magazines, empty food wrappers and that ritual pyre.

She reached deep for the little energy she had left and pushed her magic at the small pile of hot embers.

They exploded, sending little balls of fire through the small room. One landed on Trent and Nell quickly brushed if off.

Several more hit their mark, landing on Crey's back. The Sorcerer howled and fell away from the gun.

He spun on her. "That's it! I've had it with this romance-novel heroine act." His eyes were bloodshot and his shirt was covered in blood. The entire room smelled of burnt flesh. With barely a wince, he gripped the machete and ripped it out of his own shoulder.

Crey advanced on Nell. She took a step back. He raised the machete. "Now, little Halfling, you die." He glanced around the room. "Where's the fucking box?"

Nell shrugged. She'd left in the woods.

"Doesn't matter. I'll find it." He stepped closer. "Say goodbye to your girl, Prime."

"Bye-bye, baby," Trent said.

Crey took one more step—then gasped and stood stark straight, the machete still raised over his head.

His eyes bulged and his body twitched. He took a very unsteady step toward Nell before his knees gave.

The disgusting Sorcerer fell face first into the dirt. A second machete, gleaming in the light, protruded from the center of his back.

Nell looked past him to the window.

The top half of Captain Allen awkwardly protruded through the window. He gave her a large grin. "Couldn't find it in me ta leave a lady alone in the swamp. Thought I'd come check and see if you was doing okay."

Nell was immensely happy for his chivalry. She looked at the dead Sorcerer. "Good now. Thank you."

Trent looked at the newcomer. "Nice shot."

"He, um… He's been drugged," Nell said as she removed the wire from Trent's ankles and then his hands. He rubbed his wrists and stretched his shoulders but made no attempt to stand.

Captain Allen pulled himself back out the window and went around to the door. He shooed the gators back to the water before entering the hut. He looked around. "Drugged, huh?"

Trent looked up at Nell as he leaned against the post. "I'm glad you're here. We need to talk. I've figured it out." He nodded his head, a very serious look on his face. "I'm probably gonna kill you. But it'll be *me* killing you, and no one else. You hear me?" He pointed a wandering finger at her.

Captain Allen crossed his arms over his chest and nodded his approval. "Man's got a way with words, he does."

Nell grabbed the gun and Crey's cell phone then retrieved the box from the woods. By the time she returned, Trent was standing with Captain Allen's help.

Nell looked around nervously as the Captain pulled his machete from Crey's back and wiped the blood on the creep's leg. "Can we get the hell out of here?"

"Yes ma'am." He led Trent to the dock.

Nell looked back at the shack. "What about him?"

He sat Trent in one of the seats next to him on the airboat then pointed to the gators on the bank. "'Round here, nature takes its course."

She tossed the gun and phone into the water. "Ah." She nodded. "Somehow that's fitting. I'd rather not be here for dinner though."

"Me neither," Trent said, slapping his hand on his knee. "It's about time I took you out. Like a real date." He looked to Captain Allen. "You have any recommendations?"

"Not much of a restaurant man, myself."

Chapter Twelve

∞

"Please, break whatever hex the man put on him. I can't take it." Nell pleaded with Barri as the Voodoo Queen came down the stairs into the courtyard.

The beautiful woman gave her an empathetic giggle. "Is this not what you've wanted?" She turned her head in Trent's direction.

He was sitting in a chair, leaning back. A silly grin was plastered on his face as he looked up at the morning sky. "It's almost as beautiful as you, Nelly," he said.

"Not like this." Nell shook her head. "It's stopped his shift too."

Barri wrinkled her forehead in concern. "The man who did this is dead, yes?"

Nell nodded.

"Well. We have our work cut out for us. It will take me a little time to gather the necessary materials. Wait here." Barri and her aunt left, leaving Nell alone in the lovely courtyard with a very unfamiliar Trent Nicholas.

He looked over at her with a slight tilt to his head. "You think she can bring my wolf back?" His eyes had turned serious.

"He can't be gone, Trent. You just can't call him right now." Nell felt sorry for him. He'd been disoriented much of the way back to the city. When he was lucid, he kept going on about how he'd lost his other half and how Crey had killed his wolf. The cab driver offered to take them to a mental hospital.

"He's gone. It's probably for the best. I can't kill you now. You have more power than I do. I can love you and still keep you safe." He looked back to the sky. "Mi-ma said things would happen as they should."

So long Nell had waited to hear Trent accept his love for her, but the circumstances tainted the emotion. Spelled was as bad as drugged, maybe worse. The sappy adorations were nothing like what *her* Trent Nicholas would say. His ramblings were as shallow as the water in the fountain gurgling behind them.

He held out his hand. She took it, loving the feel of his fingers wrapped around hers. Would he still want to hold her hand once Barri broke the spell? Would he accept their relationship, want it, the way he had for the last few hours?

Probably not.

For a second, Nell considered letting the spell hold. Keeping him in this sappy state. Of course, that meant Trent following her around like a lovesick puppy. Not to mention the bouts of disorientation and the excruciating pain if he tried to shift.

A soft snoring sound brought her attention back to him. Trent was slouched down in the chair, face to the morning sun. He looked very peaceful. It wasn't until now that she realized he always looked tense around her.

A lone Black Witch moth landed on his chest. Nell felt comforted, and wondered how they were a comfort to her when they were wrapped up with such an evil talisman.

Mi-ma was right. Things will turn out the way they were supposed to. If he rejected her after the spell was broken, she would accept it. She simply couldn't continue the self-inflicted torture.

* * * * *

Trent woke up when he heard voices he didn't immediately recognize. Intense burning in his ears wasn't eased by holding his hands over them. He doubled over.

"What is it?" Nell was rubbing his back. He concentrated on the gentle touch of her fingers.

He took a long, deep breath. "I instinctually used my wolf senses."

"Damn." Nell kept up the rhythm of circles over his tired shoulder blades.

The Voodoo Queen approached him. "Let's see, Werewolf, if we can lift the bad mojo that evil thing put on you. We need to go into the parlor."

"Can you really do this?" he asked.

She gave him a "follow me" gesture with her head. "Auntie, lock the gates. We'll be unavailable for a while."

Heavy drapes blocked all natural light from the parlor. The furniture was old fashioned, maybe antique, but well kept. It was the kind of stuff with thin wooden legs and floral prints that always made Trent feel like it would break under his weight.

Several small groupings of candles provided all the light. A strange mixture of sage and frying oil tickled his nose, but he didn't dare try to determine the other unusual scents that his nose wanted to pick up. He breathed through his mouth.

Barri and her aunt moved a small coffee table out of the room and rolled the carpet off the floor. The old woman brought in three brooms and laid them on the floor at each entrance to the room, mumbling a chant Trent couldn't understand. Nell sat on the bottom step of the stairs.

Barri tilted her head toward the stairs. "You need to be outside the brooms, Miss Nell."

"You's gonna break the protection," Auntie said, making shooing motions with her hands. "Outside. Or up a few more stairs. And stay there 'til you is told different."

Trent stood in the middle of the floor. "Nell..." He stumbled to the couch, no longer worried about its ability to hold his weight.

Auntie came to him and urged him forward until he sat on the floor. His vision was going fuzzy. The room started to tilt. The two women began rushing around him. Nell was standing on the stairs but she hadn't crossed the boundary of the broom to come to him.

He felt liquid being poured over his head. He smelled roses, frankincense and some other floral oil. It dribbled down his forehead and over his nose and chin. He tried to wipe it away but the older woman held his hands. Fighting the urge to lash out, Trent tried to remember they were helping. Everything was fuzzy. Nell was gone. His heart started to break.

"No," he cried. "Nell!"

She wasn't gone. If he focused, he could make out her form on the stairs. But he *felt* it…felt what his body would feel if she were gone. It hurt as bad as when he'd tried to shift. Trent clenched his fists as hard as he could, felt his knuckles cracking. Tried to turn his fear and hurt into anger.

The women were chanting. Noise, thumping and screeching, was coming from all around him but he couldn't pinpoint the source. Fuzzier. More pain. He pounded his fists into the floor. His feet were numb. Copper. The taste of copper filled his mouth. A ringing started in his ears.

More pain.

More noise. Loud. Angry. Noise.

The room started to spin. Rather, Trent felt as if *he* were spinning. He was being pulled. Dragged away from this reality. He fought it, but knew he needed to let go. How?

More pain.

"Give in," a disembodied voice chanted in his brain. "Let it come."

Trent tried to relax but the searing in his joints made it impossible. The smell of burning hair panicked him. *Have to shift. Must save Nell.*

Trent tightened every muscle in his body. He strained to be as compact as he could. To ball up. Pain. More pain...

When he could take no more of the agony, he let out a soul-deep howl...and then Trent Nicholas let go. He willed every molecule in his body to relax.

And it came. The shift was awkward and slow, but it came.

The power of the spell had been cleansed. It was broken. Trent was free. He shook, stretching his muscles and feeling his wolf body. He was tired, but free of pain.

He stood shakily, trotted over and nudged Barri's hand. She was wet with sweat from her efforts.

"You'll need to stay like that for a little while." She put her hand on his head. "Let your purer essence push any remains of the hex out of your system. And you'll need lots of water and rest."

Nell approached and brushed her hand over his head. It was the first time he could remember her touching him as a wolf. She twisted her fingers into the fur around his ears. Trent wanted to shift back right then.

"I have a hotel room at the other end of the Quarter. I'll make our flight arrangements for first thing in the morning. Is that long enough?"

Auntie approached with the little scissors. "Hour or two should do it. He pushed that bugaboo out with some vigor, he did." She grabbed Trent's tail. "You mind?"

Trent didn't know what she was asking. Nell apparently did. "He won't miss a few tail feathers."

Trent whined as she cut a big chunk of hair from his tail.

"Hush. You got plenty more." She cackled and headed out of the room.

Nell put her hand on Barri's shoulder. "Thank you." Trent yipped than barked his appreciation, knowing it wasn't enough. "I'll send you some supplies from the mountains as the seasons bring them." Nell's voice was filled with sincerity.

He watched, feeling there was a deeper bond the two women were creating than even they knew. Barri had the same look on her face that the French woman had when talking to Nell on the video call.

Maybe the sexual relationships he kept assuming Nell had with all these people were all in his head.

Had he really let his jealously get to that point? He suspected he had created his own suffering. By believing so strongly he had no control over his Alpha nature, he'd manufactured things to be jealous over. Had she had crazy orgies and such during her travels, as he'd imagined? Now he suspected not. He suspected his imagination was fueled by his fears.

Trent couldn't wait to ask Nell about it. To find out what her adventures were really like. And if she told him things that made him jealous, that would be okay too. He'd deal with it. He'd find a way.

How could he have been such a fool for so long? How would he ever make it up to her?

"I would be much obliged to receive such gifts, Miss Nell Ambercroft." Barri put her hand over Nell's. "You and your name are welcome in our home anytime."

Nell looked down at him. Her eyes were red, her hair was a mess and her clothes had seen better days. Damn, she was sexy.

She had rescued him. Imagine that. Maybe that was what he'd needed all along.

* * * * *

Trent watched as Nell unpacked the items she'd purchased for them on the way to the hotel. He hadn't been happy when she'd tied him up like a common poodle outside a clothes store on Canal Street, but he knew they both needed a set of clothes for the journey home. She'd also gotten some water and protein bars.

They'd napped for a while after getting back to the room. "I'm going to shower." She looked at her watch. "Almost four hours. You're probably okay now."

He was. When he heard the shower running, Trent called forth his shift. It was smooth and painless. He stayed still in his squatted position for several moments to make sure none of the spell remained in his human form. Nothing unusual. The only pain he felt was associated with being tired and beat up.

He walked into the bathroom and pulled the shower curtain back. Nell didn't flinch. He let his gaze roam up and down her curvy body. He needed to tell her all kinds of things, but he really didn't feel much like talking at the moment.

She smiled at him. "Coming in?" She backed up, giving him room under the flow of water.

Trent accepted the invitation, stepping under the water. It was cooler than he'd expected, giving him gooseflesh. It felt great after the last two days of being out in the heat. He faced her as the water cascaded over his shoulders and down his chest.

Water turned her blonde hair darker and the curls hung thick and heavy, making interesting designs as they lay against her skin. Before he had a chance to reach for her, Nell put the flat of her hand against his chest. She looked frightened, unsure.

"Nell?"

She shook her head and bit her lip. "I don't know if I can do this anymore, Trent." She didn't look up from his chest. "This torture we put each other through."

"Nell." Trent gripped her wrist as lightly as he could, holding the connection between them. "No more torture. No more back and forth. I may have been out of my mind with that spell, but there was one thing I held on to." She looked up, met his gaze. "I love you. I can't know the future. I have no doubt you'll push me to madness at times, but I need you. I need *us*."

"What about the genetics, your concerns?"

"That's history. I can't forget it. I can be aware of it, make sure I don't make the mistakes of my fathers. I know that now. You trust me. I need to as well."

She stepped up onto the tips of her toes and pressed her lips to his. Trent thought he was going to explode with relief. He was free to love her. Free to take her as a mate.

He put his hands on her shoulders and let them slide down her back, her slick skin smooth and warm under this touch. He squeezed her ass cheeks, pulling her closer, lifting her up to deepen the kiss.

She pulled away and grabbed the soap and made a big, sloppy handful of lather, slathering it over his chest and stomach. She washed his shoulders, his arms and his hands. Her slick fingers made a trail down his abdomen and over his swelling cock. He braced himself on the tiles as her little hands squeezed him, pulling and rubbing his cock and balls until he thought he was going to burst.

She pressed her body against his, sliding from one side to the other, and transferring soap from his belly to hers, from his cock to her mound. He tingled all over from the energy in her skin. It called to him.

He couldn't take much more and the hotel tub was cramped. He needed room. "Rinse."

"Lather. Repeat?" Nell winked.

"How about rinse. Go to bed. Spread?"

He patted her dry as she stepped out of the water. There were several bruises on her body. His little Halfling had fought like a tiger for him. He couldn't be more proud of her. He kissed each of the discolored places as he dried her.

Nell walked away and Trent dropped the towel and followed, watching the sway of her ass as she approached the bed. She spun to face him and gave him a sly smile. She fell back onto the still-made bed, her legs hanging over the edge, feet barely touching the floor. She spread her legs wide, as he had suggested in the shower.

The sight of her splayed like that just about took his breath. She looked beautiful. He knelt on the floor and ran his hands over her inner thighs, from her knees to her pussy. She moaned as his fingers traced the shape of her lips. He pulled them open, further exposing her treasures.

He bent forward and dragged his tongue across the soft skin of her thigh. The taste of her made the primal part of his wolf howl in his mind. They were mated, and all this was his. Knowing he would no longer have to hold back made him harden even more.

Trent rose and swirled his tongue around her navel, teasing her belly with kisses, trailing lower.

Nell squirmed. "Trent."

Her words sounded breathless and wanting. He eased back down and then swirled his tongue around her clit, down into her opening and back up. Her scent, the sweetness of her and her longing were driving him to a pleasant insanity. He fought the urge to stop and plunge into her right that moment. He wanted to fuck her now and, at the same time, he wanted to tease her for hours.

He closed his mouth on her clit, sucking and licking. Nell groaned and lifted her upper body off the bed, resting on her elbows, watching him. The intimacy of eye contact while he lavished her pussy was incredible.

"Oh. Goddess," Nell gasped, her eyelids heavy with passion. She reached out to him, trying to grip his shoulders, to pull him to her. "Now."

"Not yet." Trent ignored her pleas.

"Trent, please." Nell's body quivered.

"Lay back. Let go." He wanted to feel her come. Wanted to make everything right for her.

Nell flopped back on the bed, her legs spread even farther. As he licked over her swollen clit she pushed her hips up, forcing the pressure to increase.

He traced her opening with his index finger. Nell was at the brink. He knew it. Trent moistened his middle finger as well and slid both into her hot pussy.

She bucked then rose back up, making eye contact again as he pumped his fingers inside her, teasing her clit with his tongue. Nell's belly tightened and he felt the flutter of her walls; they contracted around his fingers as she came. He stopped licking, nestled his head against her thigh and enjoyed the feel of her orgasm.

* * * * *

Nell fell back on the bed and two moths took flight from the headboard. "Damn."

Trent chuckled from between her legs. "Good one?" He teased her thighs with his fingertips. "I guess there's not really a bad one."

Nell nodded even if he couldn't see it from his angle. "Come up here with me," she said.

Trent climbed up her body, kissing at his leisure along the way. He scooted her back so they were both fully on the bed, if in the wrong direction for sleeping. He was between her legs, his body over hers, his erection pressing against her opening.

She reached up and traced the scar on his cheek. His ice-blue eyes were darting all over. He looked from her face to her breast to her hair and back to her eyes. He leaned in and kissed her nose, her cheek and then her eyebrows.

"Are you sure the spell's gone?" she asked.

He kissed her lightly on the lips. "Yes." His lips brushed hers again. "No need to worry." A third time, kissing her with the lightest of touches. "I know you won't trust this right away." He kissed her chin again. "But I promise. No more pulling away."

He leaned down and drew a nipple into his mouth, sucking just hard enough to make her squirm. Nell arched into the feeling. His body was hot. His weight was comforting, reassuring. Nell felt as if he was truly with her for the first time. She spread her legs wider in invitation.

He moved to the other nipple. She shifted her hips again and the head of his cock pushed the smallest bit inside her. He groaned. The vibration tingled on her nipple.

"Nelly." He pushed farther into her, his face nuzzling her neck, his arms around her—then all movement stopped.

Nell panicked. "What is it?"

He looked back up to her. "Nothing. I wanted to feel you, to be wrapped around you and inside you." He kissed her chin once more. "Savoring."

Nell realized she was waiting for the other shoe to drop, for him to decide he wasn't capable of being her mate again. She slipped her hands around his waist and hugged him back. Holding him close, clinging.

"I'm sorry, Nelly. I love you. I have loved you for years. I want this." He kissed her again. This time he plunged his tongue in her mouth and explored. He began to thrust, and not soft and steady. He drove into her. He wrapped his arms around her, holding her as close as possible. He pulled his lips from hers and buried his face in her neck.

The feel of him sliding in and out, taking her, felt like the wolf, like passion. She tried to meet each thrust, to give back. His skin was on fire. His hair teased her cheek. She gripped his back, dug her nails into his skin. She was going to come again.

His teeth closed on her shoulder. The sting made her clench, both her nails and her pussy, as he thrust in again.

He groaned and bucked.

Nell climaxed. She grabbed his ass and pulled him closer. Trying to hold him still.

"Too close. Can't." He pushed one last time and growled. The veins in his neck pulsed with his orgasm. He slid in and out another time or two, his eyes closed.

Nell put her palms on his cheeks and pulled him into a kiss.

A kiss that said she trusted him, and understood everything.

* * * * *

Trent held up the box as she finished in the bathroom. They had two hours until they left New Orleans to meet with a Council member back in the mountains. "It doesn't feel so evil anymore."

Nell pulled her shirt over her head. "That's because it's empty." She opened a door and punched in a code on the safe in the closet. When it popped open, she lifted the talisman out. "Barri cleansed it to keep it from attracting every evil thing in the city. But I was afraid to take it out to the swamp. That's why I got the hotel room in the first place." She set the necklace on the desk.

"You bartered for my life with an empty box?" He looked a little surprised.

"Well…" Nell put her hands on her hips. "Would you rather I took it out there and let Crey get it?"

He looked from her to the balcony and back. "I guess not."

He went out onto the balcony and sat in one of the big iron chairs. Nell followed and curled up in his lap, her head on his shoulder, loving the solid feel of his body holding hers.

"Crey was talking to someone on the phone back in that hut," she said.

"The Council will figure out who helped Crey. We won't need to worry once they have the talisman." He pushed an errant curl from her face. "They'll want to start with why your father had such a strong talisman in his belongings."

Nell shrugged against his shoulder. "He was a collector. Goddess knows what might be in all those boxes in the basement." She thought on it for a moment. She really didn't want the Council members poking their noses into her life. "You're the Prime. Won't you be the one investigating?"

He shook his head. "After we turn that thing in..." Trent gently kissed her on the forehead and then looked down the street. "How about we do some of that traveling you like so much?"

Nell leaned away from his chest so she could look in his eyes. "What? You're not going after these guys yourself?" Part of her still feared he might use that chase as an excuse to turn tail and run away from her.

"Nah. Crey hired local goons to do his work here. I figure he was stealing or begging spells and power amulets from a master. Someone else can handle that. I have my own objective now." His hand rubbed a loose circle on her back. "To stay with you. You need protecting. Just in case."

"Right." She crinkled up her nose.

"I think it's time for a big change." Trent smiled at her. "After we deliver this thing, I'm taking some time off. I want to make up for what we've missed. What I made us miss."

Nell leaned back against his chest. "I like the sound of change."

Epilogue

ᎷᏎ

"So it wasn't a diamond?" Sonja asked.

"Nope." Nell looked at the box sitting on her old, nicked-up kitchen table. At the moment it seemed impossible that so much trouble had come from one simple wooden box. The calming mojo Barri had put on it still seemed to be in effect. The dark chunk of wood didn't feel oppressive. "Barri found out it was some kind of rare African crystal. It holds the magic of the box. No giant diamond for us." It was a shame too. That would have been a great boon for the family coffers.

"Why do you think that Crey guy went to all the trouble to get it?" Sonja chose the chair farthest from the box and sat leaning as far back as possible, even though no blood magic emanated from it at the moment.

Trent came in and slid his arms around Nell's waist, pulling her back against his chest. He kissed the top of her head. Sonja gave Nell a raised eyebrow and a knowing smile. Nell couldn't stop her own happy grin. The trip home had been wonderful. He was attentive, light and, well — not Trent Nicholas the Prime at all. Nell liked it.

"I think it was the power boost." Trent picked the box up and moved it over to a small antique desk beside the back door, as if to get it away from them all. It looked like a simple curio, sitting between a potted ivy and a ceramic purple owl. He pulled a chair out for Nell and headed for the counter to get a pitcher of tea.

"Jeez-Louise, you should have heard the lovely, flirty things he whispered to me on the way out of that swamp." She winked at Sonja. "Promised me we'd have five kids and get one of those big summer houses over on Lake Johnson."

"What?" He poured her tea. "I said no such thing."

Nell nodded to Sonja, ignoring Trent's denial. "Promised me he'd paint my toenails a different shade of pink every week *and* give me foot massages to make up for being such an ass."

Sonja giggled. Trent scowled.

Nell propped her elbow on the table and put her chin on her fist. "Even said he'd do all the house work when he moved in here."

"Nell."

"Ooh. He's using the Alpha voice." Sonja wiggled her fingers.

He handed Sonja a glass. "We have *not* decided which house we're moving into."

Yeah. Nell knew the pack had to be considered. Still. It was so easy to rattle him over his lack of memory. And fun. She wasn't going to let him off the hook too soon. After all, he'd tormented her for years. Kind of.

Nell consoled him with a light pat on the forearm. "Yes we have, baby. We decided in the swamp." He rolled his eyes. She turned back to Sonja, dismissing his reaction to the conversation. "Crey could have admitted to the Kennedy assassination that night and Trent wouldn't remember. He has to take my word on everything."

He ran his fingers through that thick hair of his and shook his head. "I never want to be that out of control again. My guess is that Crey was trying to increase his own power for something. That's what the necklace is for, after all. But if he shared any details...who knows? I can't remember. And the local Prime cleaned the scene right away. There's no trace of him in the swamp and no clue to where he lived. Whatever he wanted, he's no longer a threat, thanks to Captain Allen and his mean machete."

Nell nodded. She would be grateful for that man for the rest of her life.

Sonja looked back at the box. "So when is Councilman Sanderson showing up for it?"

"Tomorrow." Nell put a hand on Trent's leg. Now that she had her wolf and her life was no longer in danger, she wasn't as hesitant to give the ugly thing up. She smiled at him before gazing back at Sonja. "Maybe you and Trina and I should go through all those boxes in the basement and make sure Dad didn't leave us any other big surprises." There would surely be a treasure trove of trinkets and amulets down there. Even though she knew most were just antiquities, collectables from preternatural history, there could be something else dangerous. If so, she wanted it out. "Mi-ma and Trent can help."

Trent shook his head. "I'll be in Dallas."

"What?" Nell drew her brows in. "That's outside your jurisdiction."

"Maybe Tokyo. The farther the better. If you three Halfling are playing with unknown magic, I want to get as far away as possible."

Trent winked and Nell chuckled. This was the way life should be. She finally had everything she wanted. Home, family—and her wolf.

Also by Mari Freeman

ℰℭ

eBooks:

Beware of the Cowboy

Birthright

Cougar Challenge 6: Sin on Skin

Hot, Hard & Hexing

Hot, Hard & Howling

Love Doctor

Print Books:

Birthright

Cougar Challenge: Tease the Cougar

Plan for Pleasure *(anthology)*

About the Author

෨

Mari Freeman lives, disguised as a normal suburbanite, in central North Carolina. When not penning romantic erotica, she enjoys horses, hiking, traveling, good food and friends. An outdoors girl at heart, you can often find her at the lake with laptop fired up, fishing line in the water and her imagination running wild.

In her previous lives, she's held an interesting array of occupations. She's been a project manager, a software-testing manager, sold used cars, pumped gas at a truck stop and worked in a morgue.

Mari's favorite stories include Alpha females in love with even more Alpha males. She finds the clash of passionate, strong-willed personalities fascinating. She writes contemporary, paranormal and a little science fiction/fantasy.

෨

The author welcomes comments from readers. You can find her website and email address on her author bio page at www.ellorascave.com.

Tell Us What You Think

We appreciate hearing reader opinions about our books. You can email us at Comments@EllorasCave.com.

Why an electronic book?

We live in the Information Age — an exciting time in the history of human civilization, in which technology rules supreme and continues to progress in leaps and bounds every minute of every day. For a multitude of reasons, more and more avid literary fans are opting to purchase e-books instead of paper books. The question from those not yet initiated into the world of electronic reading is simply: *Why?*

1. *Price.* An electronic title at Ellora's Cave Publishing runs anywhere from 40% to 75% less than the cover price of the exact same title in paperback format. Why? Basic mathematics and cost. It is less expensive to publish an e-book (no paper and printing, no warehousing and shipping) than it is to publish a paperback, so the savings are passed along to the consumer.

2. *Space.* Running out of room in your house for your books? That is one worry you will never have with electronic books. For a low one-time cost, you can purchase a handheld device specifically designed for e-reading. Many e-readers have large, convenient screens for viewing. Better yet, hundreds of titles can be stored within your new library — on a single microchip. There are a variety of e-readers from different manufacturers. You can also read e-books on your PC or laptop computer. (Please note that Ellora's Cave does not endorse any specific brands.

You can check our website at www.ellorascave.com for information we make available to new consumers.)

3. *Mobility.* Because your new e-library consists of only a microchip within a small, easily transportable e-reader, your entire cache of books can be taken with you wherever you go.

4. *Personal Viewing Preferences.* Are the words you are currently reading too small? Too large? Too... ANNOYING? Paperback books cannot be modified according to personal preferences, but e-books can.

5. *Instant Gratification.* Is it the middle of the night and all the bookstores near you are closed? Are you tired of waiting days, sometimes weeks, for bookstores to ship the novels you bought? Ellora's Cave Publishing sells instantaneous downloads twenty-four hours a day, seven days a week, every day of the year. Our webstore is never closed. Our e-book delivery system is 100% automated, meaning your order is filled as soon as you pay for it.

Those are a few of the top reasons why electronic books are replacing paperbacks for many avid readers.

As always, Ellora's Cave welcomes your questions and comments. We invite you to email us at Comments@ellorascave.com or write to us directly at Ellora's Cave Publishing Inc., 1056 Home Avenue, Akron, OH 44310-3502.

MAKE EACH DAY MORE *EXCITING* WITH OUR

ELLORA'S
CAVEMEN
CALENDAR

✝ WWW.ELLORASCAVE.COM ✝

ELLORA'S CAVE
Romanticon

Annual convention for women who refuse to behave

Discover for yourself why readers can't get enough
of the multiple award-winning publisher
Ellora's Cave.

Whether you prefer e-books or paperbacks,

be sure to visit EC on the web at
www.ellorascave.com

for an erotic reading experience that will leave you
breathless.

CPSIA information can be obtained at www.ICGtesting.com
Printed in the USA
BVOW071918041211

277505BV00001B/16/P